DOOM ANGEL

H. DAVID BLALOCK

THE ANGELKILLER TRIAD

BOOK ONE
ANGELKILLER

BOOK TWO
TRAITOR ANGEL

BOOK THREE
DOOM ANGEL

DOOM ANGEL

H. DAVID BLALOCK

SEVENTH STAR PRESS

Cover art and illustrations: Matthew Perry
Cover art and illustrations in this book copyright ©
2014 Matthew Perry & Seventh Star Press, LLC.

Editor: Amanda DcBord

Published by Seventh Star Press, LLC.

ISBN Number: 978-1-937929-55-8

Seventh Star Press
www.seventhstarpress.com
info@seventhstarpress.com

Publisher's Note:
Doom Angel is a work of fiction. All names,
characters, and places are the product of the
author's imagination, used in fictitious manner. Any
resemblances to actual persons, places, locales,
events, etc. are purely coincidental.

Printed in the United States of America

First Edition

DEDICATION

For the Knights,
the Angelkillers,
and all those who resist.
You know who you are.

PROLOGUE

Why do bad things happen to good people? The answer to that question is as simple as it is difficult to accept.

In the beginning, there was a war.

The Master's first creations, the angelic hordes, became divided when He brought into being yet another race and world. There began a conflict between those who felt the Master had abandoned them and those who remained loyal. The Enemy wanted control over the new creation, believing himself to be more worthy. The war raged for time immemorial, neither side gaining advantage. Then, the Dark took a daring step and opted to involve Men in the struggle. As a result the Dark gained an unwitting ally, the very creation for which the combatants struggled.

Forbidden to harm Man by the Master Himself, the Angels of Light were forced to retreat and The Enemy won by default what they had coveted for so long. But the victory came with an unexpected cost.

In order to retain their prize, the Dark found it had to deceive Man into believing he had fought for the right side, the side that upheld the Master and His Plan. The Dark had to convince Man he had fought for the Light, and that the Light won.

But there are those who have learned the truth and fight to right the heinous wrong wreaked on Humanity, to defeat the Dark and manifest the real victory of the Master: the bringing of Light into the world. These fighters originally were few, and by Grace were given long life and wisdom. They received the name Angelkillers for their faithfulness to the Conflict. Each built a cell of followers until, over the years, a new force appeared.

Called simply The Army and sworn to secrecy out of necessity, they lived in the shadows and struck at The Enemy when the opportunity arose. Under certain circumstances, an Army fighter would be raised to the station of a Knight, whose power was second only to an Angel. When a situation was particularly critical to the Conflict's advancement, a Knight would be dispatched to tip the balance. For more than one Knight to appear was historical. For three to appear at a time indicated impending events of apocalyptic proportion.

Jonah Mason was an Angelkiller and head of one of the

cells of the North American Army resistance. For centuries, he had fought the growing secular atmosphere of a nation losing its soul to the materialistic and cynical influence of The Enemy.

He and his group faced down the Minion Azazel, a minor demon inhabiting the body of a man named Michael Jenkins, who was in the employ of a mysterious Enemy agent known only as Andreal. They did this at the request of another Minion whose name was Dorian Azrael, the head of a global corporation, Andlat Enterprises. Certain files had gone missing and needed to be recovered immediately. Mason and his group were able to recover them by breaking into and destroying the computer system of one of Andlat Enterprises' subsidiaries, Catalina Industries.

There had been reservations about working for Azrael, about siding with The Enemy even if it was against another Minion. Mason had overridden those reservations, and in so doing had involved them in an intrigue they began to suspect involved much more than just the rebellion of one Minion against another.

The most disturbing part of this event, however, was not that Mason had to face a Minion, but that three Knights had appeared, ostensibly to support him.

Though one of the cell's number, Harold Martin, was

hospitalized from an earlier encounter with agents of the Minion Azazel, and two others, Stephen Overguard and Janice Meeker, were not to take part in the final battle, Mason drew the demon out and faced it down with the aid of the Knights. However, in so doing they unwittingly awoke in John Tripp, Mason's oldest ally, a previously unsuspected problem. Tripp, unbeknownst to the rest, witnessed the appearance of a Seraph, one of the most powerful of the Angels of Light, at the end of the battle during the Minion's exorcism. His Puritan background rose up from its long-forgotten place in the back of his mind, and he became obsessed with seeing it again, no matter the cost.

Mason himself was faced with a choice after the battle. It became clear the reason so many Knights had appeared was not just because the Minion had to be put down, but because Mason, an Angelkiller, had made a deal with Dorian Azrael, an agent of The Enemy. The Knights were not impressed by his reasoning or excuses, and Mason now faced an ultimatum that would strike to his very soul.

Personal problems aside, the Conflict raged on. It became necessary to deal with an executive of one of The Enemy's companies when they were discovered hacking into the company computer system. That executive was Andrew Nicholson, who the cell soon realized was the mysterious

Andreal himself. Nicholson was keen to reacquire the files before the cell returned them to Azrael, and set up a meeting.

Nicholson became an unwilling ally as The Enemy saw his independent negotiations with Mason and his cell as a betrayal. An assassin was sent to kill him, an attempt which failed but left Nicholson wounded. Mason reluctantly accepted him into the cell rather than abandon him to The Enemy, and Nicholson's actions seemed to show he could be trusted.

Perhaps.

Meanwhile, Tripp announced he wished to retire, to spend the rest of his days contemplating his vision of the Seraph; Martin was caught up in The Enemy VR after his abduction, being interrogated about the whereabouts of the missing files; and Overguard's feelings for Meeker caused friction between him and Nicholson.

The cell was on the brink of shattering, and the final confrontation with Dorian Azrael was yet to come.

1

"If we're going to get him back, we need to get into Andlat."

The remaining members of the little Army cell had gathered in the front room of the cabin to plan their next move. Before anything else, they wanted to rescue Martin, but a debate had developed over exactly how to go about it.

"There doesn't seem to be much more we can do," Jaelon said as she gazed at the I/O device she held. The virtual reality interface they were using was light-years ahead of commercial technology, enabling them to bypass the majority of the security measures used by Andlat Enterprises.

Long ago she had been a Pictish warrior, but now she was a Knight in the service of their Master. Her dark hair and glittering eyes marked her as a beauty in any age, but the grimness of her visage belied her sense of purpose. "With the central computer damaged, we have no real way to get in."

"Not through the VR, anyway," Populus agreed. The slightly built Greek Knight had a disarming personality and a jovial mien, but underneath that was the quick intellect and cunning of a master tactician.

Mason, the leader of the Army cell, tossed his interface device onto the table. "Well, then, we do it the old-fashioned way."

All eyes turned to him.

"We go after the Director personally," Mason went on.

"Are you out of your mind?" Nicholson objected. The former CFO of Catalina Industries had been pressed into service with the Army when he fell afoul of Azrael. Only now was he beginning to understand what that meant. "I know him. I know what he can do, the resources he can use. You have a better chance of spitting into a hurricane and staying dry."

Populus snickered at that, then shrugged when Nicholson gave him a dirty look.

"Look, we know he must be in trouble with his own superiors by now," Mason explained. "With the loss of Catalina Industries' main computer and the breakdown in his security, he's as vulnerable as he's ever going to be."

"I don't know," Overguard put in. The big Texan had a bluff personality that turned morose easily. "Even crippled, he's pretty formidable. Are you sure you want to chance losing this entire cell just to get one Minion?"

"Stephen has a point, Mason," Meeker agreed. She smiled at Overguard. Their connection was well known in the group. Although she was the newest to the cell, the others had already come to accept her as one of their own. "Wouldn't it make more sense to be content with what we've already done? I mean, look, his major operations are shut down, the majority of his infrastructure is in a shambles. How much is enough?"

Mason looked at the Cypriot Knight Malthusan. He was a huge man, a former mercenary who had seen service in battles going back hundreds of years. If there was anyone who could gauge the need for combat, it would be he. The Knight took the hint and spoke.

"Azrael is a linchpin," the big man said, ignoring the thrum of the cabin wards at the pronunciation of the name. The wards were put in place as protection from unseen forces and reacted to the presence or summoning of an Enemy. "If we can unseat him, we remove a key part of The Enemy's hold on humanity. The deception that The Enemy uses to keep mankind under its thumb is based on finances and politics. Those are the avenues we must use. We have to shift the power in those two arenas from The Enemy to The Master. I doubt anyone on the outside will realize what has happened, but the difference will slowly manifest itself over the years.

"The Enemy worked for millennia to gain control and is deeply entrenched. It has taken centuries for us to get this far, but we have much farther to go. We are fighting a battle in a larger war, one that we can still lose in spite of the gains we have made." Malthusan looked at Jaelon. "The three of us were sent to help, to reinforce what you might do, but the direction of that action must come from you."

It was the most they had heard from Malthusan since the Knights joined the group, and it was a little unsettling to hear the situation outlined in that deep bass voice. Silence fell over them as the cell considered their options.

"If you are content with what you have accomplished, we are willing to accept that," Jaelon said at last. "But ask yourselves this: is he hurt enough he cannot recover? Given enough time, could he not regain what he lost?"

Mason watched as each of the others thought about Jaelon's question. Overguard scowled and uncrossed his arms. Meeker chewed on her thumbnail and stared into space. Nicholson, shaking his head, mumbled something inaudible.

"Wait! There is one thing everyone seems to have forgotten," Populus stepped forward to say. His face was ashen and he looked shaken. "Something either we have been blinded against, or conveniently neglected to remember."

They looked at each other and him in confusion.

"Exactly *who* is he in the Hierarchy?" Populus asked pointedly.

A silence settled over them until Jaelon gasped.

"How could we forget?" she stammered.

"What? What did we forget?" Meeker said, alarmed.

The truth crashed in on Mason at that moment. How indeed? It was something they should have remembered from the beginning. It made sense, though, that they would forget. If they had recalled the truth, they would never have agreed to work for the Minion.

"Traditionally," Mason said, "Azrael is the name of the Angel of Death."

The wards shivered again.

"You're not seriously suggesting this man is an incarnation of...?" Meeker asked, her voice shaking a little.

"No, the real Angel obeys only our Master's commands," Jaelon told her. "The Enemy may like to believe otherwise, but I assure you that is not the case."

"But any Minion that would dare to compare itself to that entity, even simply by name, must be extremely powerful,"

Mason observed soberly.

"Not to mention supremely confident in his own position and ability," Populus grimly added.

They all considered that for a moment.

"Okay, granted Azrael is formidable," Mason said, setting the wards humming again, "it changes nothing. We have to find out how to take him down. We know the elimination of Catalina Industries crippled his operations in the Americas, but Andlat Enterprises is a global entity with almost limitless resources. It won't be long before he recovers and we're right back where we started."

"Actually, we'll be worse off," Overguard glumly put in. "Thanks to the infiltration of our communication network, we have no secure way to contact Central any more. We're cut off."

"True enough," Populus said. "However, with some time I believe I can finish the work Martin started before he was taken."

Mason sighed. They had lost Chandler early on, then Martin. John Tripp, his oldest friend and the last person in the room, sat gazing vacantly into the fireplace. For all intents, he was gone from them as well. He barely spoke any more, spending his time inside his own head, reliving those last few moments when Jenkins had been exorcised and he caught a fleeting glimpse of an actual Seraph. He was wrapped up in his obsession with that vision.

The thought of the Master's attending angel sent shivers along his spine. He hadn't seen but a hint of what drove the Minion out of Michael Jenkins, but that hint still terrified and thrilled him. It was so different from the vision of the Cherub he had at the siege of Acre.

He should have died there in the back and forth of the battle, caught between the hostile city and the marauding hordes of Saladin's troops. Mason wore the colors of the Order of Montjoy then, although its red and white cross was ragged and torn from the battle at Hattin. Nearly the entire contingent had been destroyed there, so he'd attached himself to a group who maintained they were from the Order of Santiago, which he doubted at the time. More than one titled lord died on that bloody field at Acre, but it was the arrival of the Cherub after the death of Gerard de Ridefort, the Grand Master of the Templars, that helped turn the tide. Although unseen by the mundane eyes of the haggard friendly forces, the Cherub's influence was evident in their determination and fervor after suffering losses counting in the thousands.

That apparition had reassured him the Master had not forsaken them. How could he have forgotten that until now?

Clearly, the intervening years had dulled the memory, but such a sight should not have been forgotten at all. It should be a constant source of inspiration. Was there something wrong with him, that he should have misplaced or suppressed the memory? Or had he done it to avoid becoming as distracted and obsessed as Tripp now was? The effect on his friend was profound, and he could sense a distance developing between Tripp and the rest of the cell, a gulf growing wider daily.

It was ironic. When all this began, when Azrael had first approached them about recovering the files Jenkins stole, they had all been strangers to him except Tripp. Now that they had the files, Jenkins was dead, Azazel banished, and Catalina Industries eliminated, Tripp was becoming the stranger while he grew to know the others more.

It was not what he considered a fair trade.

"Do what you can," he told Populus. "Until we can rescue Martin..."

"If he's still alive," Overguard gloomed.

"...we'll need someone to take his place," Mason finished, ignoring the Texan.

"Do you really think he's dead?" Meeker asked Overguard.

The big man shrugged. "I dunno."

"If they wanted him dead, they could have killed him in

Tennessee," Jaelon pointed out, referring to when Martin was kidnapped.

"Maybe he would have been better off," Overguard grumbled.

"What do you mean?" Meeker asked.

"He means," Malthusan rumbled, "Minions only take captives if they want something from them, and they will use any means to get it. It means Mr. Martin is being put to the ultimate test." Malthusan took a breath and glared at Mason. "Let us hope he can find the strength to withstand it."

* * *

Knight Maachen jumped aside as the beast charged, moving quickly even under the weight of his heavy armor. He was thrilled to his soul at the strength surging through previously immobilized limbs. He reveled at the freedom in his legs, rejoiced at the heaviness gone, exulted at the life coursing through them. He lifted the shield strapped to his left arm and swung the longsword in a slow circle toward his opponent.

He was no longer Harold Martin, the computer expert for Mason's Army cell. That man had been wounded, beaten, and kidnapped – unable to flee when his captors appeared at the west Tennessee house he and Mason's cell used as a headquarters, bound to the wheelchair because his legs hadn't healed from the burns he suffered when Azazel's men torched his own house. He hadn't let his disability stop him then, had refused to stop doing his part for the Master. Now, he knew who he really was in the Conflict. He had been given a Vision, the revelation of his office in the Master's service.

The beast's thirty-foot long bulk flashed by unnaturally fast, the spikes running the length of its back shivering with each movement. Maachen circled it slowly, keeping his shield between them. Its size didn't bother him. It was the stench and heat of its breath that portended worse. The head at the end of its sinuous neck swayed above him, lidless eyes gazing at him with nothing but hatred behind the vertical slits of their pupils.

"You cannot win, Martin," the woman standing beside the beast growled. "Tell us what we want to know, and we will make your death quick and painless."

The cold in her eyes had not shifted at all. In spite of everything, Maachen felt sorry for her in a way. She looked like a regular person, whatever her real nature, and her outward beauty should have tempered that steely gaze. She wasn't able to make him talk while he was trapped in the wheelchair, locked in a featureless room with armed guards hanging over him, so she had brought him here, telling him it was the world first created, the home of The Enemy himself. But when he had seen himself outfitted in the armor from the MMORPG virtual reality used by the Army for communications before its compromise, he knew the truth. It was simply another VR environment, complex and intimidating psychologically, fitted undoubtedly with the latest interface technology. The beast might be nothing more than a computerized construct, a figment of imagination, but the impact of interacting with it through the interface would wreak physical effects. The pain, the wounds inflicted, even death in this reality would be mirrored on his real self, wherever it might be.

Still in all, she hadn't been able to make him talk before. Did she really think she could make him talk now?

But he didn't have time to worry about her. The beast was maneuvering around him, its body giving off heat in waves carrying the scent of decay and waste and rot. In his heart, Maachen knew he couldn't win this fight, but that didn't stop him from determination to give it his all. The Master called him to this Conflict. He would honor that call, no matter the cost.

It was his duty, and it was right.

The beast gathered itself for another lunge. He brought his shield and weapon to bear. He wouldn't avoid it this time.

He was going to end this, one way or another.

* * *

Mason stood looking out over the cliff into the distance. He had pulled a black sweater and denim trousers over his six foot, three inch, solid frame. Far below, the White River rolled tranquilly past. Behind him, the smell of cooking wafted from the three-room cabin the cell was now using as a headquarters since the loss of Mason's Tennessee house. He guessed Janice Meeker was trying to make something of the dried victuals stored in the cabin. Outside, the air was thick with the scent of the surrounding greenery. The murmur of voices inside was nearly covered by the singing of the redbirds and the cawing of a jay somewhere nearby. A hummingbird chattered as it sped by his head toward the feeder hanging under the cabin's front window. He could hear the Knights moving around in their van. While his own group used the cabin, the Knights slept in their vehicle, a large paneled van fitted with a dazzling array of devices and an impressive armory of non-lethal weaponry.

The cabin wasn't safe anymore. The Enemy might not know their exact position, but the fact they had found them at that bar in Mountain Home meant they were closing in. The meeting they had arranged with Nicholson had gone wrong when Nicholson's secretary shot and wounded Nicholson in full view of everyone at the bar. Jaelon had barely escaped being killed herself in the ensuing struggle with the shooter, but they were able to spirit Nicholson away before the assassin could finish the job.

He lit a Montecristo and drew heavily on it, savoring its taste before sending a cloud of thick smoke out over the edge.

He needed to move the cell again. But where? None of the others had isolated locations they might use. They needed to find a place away from the general population, but not so far they couldn't get access to the networks. They also required an anonymous workstation, one Andlat Enterprises couldn't track, but Azrael's resources were too numerous and sophisticated to be sure they could find one. Populus had told him there was tracking code everywhere he went online. Only the Greek Knight's talents kept them from being discovered.

As if summoned by his thoughts, Populus stepped up beside him. The Knight stretched his wiry frame and took a deep breath. Populus had taken over as their computer technician when Martin was kidnapped. Mason was constantly amazed at the man's technical acumen in spite of his age. His intellectual adaptability had proved invaluable in the past few days. They could never have recovered from the loss of Martin without him. It was Populus who set up the electronic camouflage net protecting them from detection by the megaplex security drones that passed overhead regularly. For extra security he had also rigged the cabin for power from the van, isolating it from the national grid power line hanging above them.

Populus nodded to no one in particular and smiled. "Beautiful view," the Knight observed. "In many ways, it reminds me of home."

Mason grunted his agreement. Now that it was pointed out, he saw the truth behind that. The high location, the river below, the forested surroundings... It was almost an exact duplicate of the place his mentor had used as a base, the place he had first become aware of the Conflict and the Truth behind it. The memory was a pleasant ache in his chest.

The men stood quietly enjoying the vista for several moments, each caught up in thought, before Populus cleared his throat.

"We need to get inside Andlat itself," Populus told him without turning from the view. "With one of their internal stations, I can more easily shut down their systems, perhaps for good."

"And how, exactly, do we go about doing that?" he asked with a chuckle.

Populus grimaced. "We find someone on the inside, or go

in ourselves."

"None of us can go in. They know us all by now."

The Knight did look at him then. "There is a way."

He raised an eyebrow in question.

"Nicholson."

"Ah," he said, drawing again on the cigar and exhaling slowly as he thought. "I see."

"For all intents and purposes, Azrael believes Nicholson is dead, killed in the bar."

Mason contemplated the end of the smoke. "Maybe, maybe not. One way or the other, they'll be suspicious when he shows up alive," he pointed out.

"Of course. But I think they'll take him back anyway."

"Why would they?"

Populus grinned. "The Enemy prides itself on its ability to deceive and betray. I believe they will take Nicholson back so they might use him against us."

"A double agent?"

"Yes. They will allow him full access and watch him closely, expecting he will betray them to us. They will set a trap for us using him as bait."

He shook his head. "Too risky. You're taking too much for granted."

"Am I? They planted an agent in his office before. No doubt she was monitoring his communications with us. That has to be how they found out about the meeting at the bar. It worked for them once. You don't think they'll try it again?"

He frowned. The risk could be worth the reward. There was one thing, though. "Nicholson could be killed," he objected.

"There is that," Populus agreed. "So, it must be his decision."

Mason drew thoughtfully on his Montecristo. Populus had a logical mind. He trusted the Greek's judgment when it came to technology, but he preferred Jaelon's advice on strategy. She had demonstrated an insight that looked past emotion and surface appearances when it came to the methods and motives of The Enemy. Of all the other Knights, she had the most personal experience in direct contact with The Enemy. Her time as a Roman slave and later as the Knight Clement's disciple gave her knowledge of The Enemy most closely matching his own. Malthusan obviously trusted her implicitly. The big Cypriot followed her without question. His military background obviously made it easier for him to accept her as his commander. Even Populus deferred to her more often than not, though his reasons were more obscure.

"Have you discussed this with Jaelon?" Mason asked.

"I have."

"What's her take on it?"

"She thinks it risky but is willing to try it."

Mason nodded slowly. So, that question was answered. There was a critical one left. "Let's assume Nicholson agrees and everything goes as you say. How does this get us into Andlat's systems?"

The Knight produced a small container. Flipping it open, he revealed a tiny metal case about three millimeters on a side.

"There are ten microdots in here," he said. "Each contains a metatoroidal worm."

"A what kind of worm?"

"It's a potent digital virus. Just one microdot introduced to any electronic or biological interface will infect the entire network in a few nanoseconds."

"A digital bomb?"

"Faster and deadlier, because it can replicate and attack specific targets."

"A smart digital bomb, then."

"Indeed," Populus said. "It infects and remains invisible while propagating in the operating system. Once fully integrated, it..."

Mason raised a hand to stop. How it worked didn't matter

to him. He just needed to know one thing. "You're sure it will work?"

Populus snapped the lid shut. "Nothing is sure in this world. However, I am confident this has the best chance of success."

Mason flicked ash and grunted. "We'll only get one chance at this."

"I know."

"Their IT people aren't slackers. They may have a defense in place against this kind of thing already," he pointed out.

"Possible, but I doubt it."

Mason eyed him. "Do you?"

"I do, since I designed this myself. If their heuristic defenses are quick and smart enough to catch this, I would be very surprised and impressed."

Mason studied the box for a moment, then looked at the Knight. There were so many things that could go wrong with this. Populus was brilliant, but The Enemy was not to be underestimated. Mason and his cell had been successful in so much recently. He attributed that to the Master and His grace in sending the Knights. Was he being ungrateful by doubting the outcome of this latest plan?

When it came right down to it, he felt responsible for the

others, even the Knights to some extent. He had been the leader for so long it was difficult not to feel that way. The Knights had already told him he was being overprotective and reminded him that he was not personally responsible for the lives of his cell companions. They had pressed him to move on, to allow the others the chance to grow on their own. Tripp was retiring, Martin had disappeared, Chandler was dead. Was it his fault they ended up that way? Had he crippled their decision making, indirectly causing them to go down an unintended path because of his need to protect them?

Perhaps it was time he stopped standing in their way. Maybe it was time he let someone else choose their path, and let them deal with the consequences themselves.

"Let's talk to Nicholson," he said. "After we've had something to eat."

* * *

Andlat Enterprises' tentacles stretched deep into the Persian Empire. In fact, if it wasn't for Andlat there would be no Empire at all, just the endlessly bickering tribal nations that, unchanged and unchanging, had inhabited the Middle and Near East for millennia. Agents personally chosen by Dorian Azrael had worked for decades coaxing, coercing, negotiating, even assassinating to forward his goal. To Azrael, everything and everyone was a tool to be used toward the satisfaction of his ambition. No impediment was allowed to slow or stop him. No treachery was too low, no betrayal too heinous if it furthered his plan. A plan whose ultimate outcome would place him in the position of being the most powerful being on the planet.

Through it all, he was careful to maintain a public image as a philanthropist of the first order. To the outside world he was a figure to be admired and exalted, a statesman trying to bring an end to war, famine, and disease. His standing in the international community was unquestioned.

A situation which was a source of constant amusement to him.

Azrael sat at the head of the conference table and glared at the subordinates arrayed on either side of its length. The command and control network for the Persian Imperial forces was working perfectly, but Azrael knew better than to drop vigilance until the campaign reached its current goal: the total subjugation of the European Bloc.

He ruled Andlat Enterprises with an iron fist, as he had always done with the hundreds of organizations he had helmed over the centuries. The lackeys cowering around him were loyal only as long as they believed he was the power behind Andlat.

Should any of them think they might have the leverage, they would undoubtedly turn on him as Nicholson and Azazel had done. That episode had been dealt with in a most satisfying manner using agents of the opposition to do the dirty work. The results hadn't been exactly what he expected, but nothing in this life ever worked out perfectly. He accepted Azazel's demise and Nicholson's extermination as necessary to the fruition of his plan. Unlike most of his kind, Azrael was adaptable, or at least flexible.

In spite of all that, he felt the pressure from his own master as keenly as these toadies felt their fear of him. He fully intended that these underlings would share in his discomfort. All the better to insure their continued obedience.

He rose to stand and glower at them from his full height of six and a half feet. The subordinates' seats were set lower than his own by strategic design, forcing them to look up ever so slightly at him, even when he was seated. A team of psychologists had worked for months to set this atmosphere, to afford him a physical and subconscious preeminence.

"We are at a critical juncture," he announced, the carefully crafted acoustics of the chamber giving his already bass voice a thundering timbre from one end to the other of the table. "Within a few days, war will burn across Europe. The Imperial forces will sweep into Iberia and then launch through the North African Bloc. Already we are preparing for a strike against the Far Eastern Bloc and by this time next year the Empire will stretch from the Atlantic to the Pacific, from the pole to the Indian Ocean."

A polite smattering of applause sputtered from his sycophants. He allowed it for a few moments before continuing.

"This world has too long been subject to petty squabbling and jingoistic stupidity. Only a single world government can effectively end world hunger, stop poverty, and give us the resources to finally conquer disease. Only a one world government can guarantee world peace and you, gentlemen, are the visionaries who will bring that about!"

The applause this time was more enthusiastic. He smiled at them and their applause picked up in volume. Their relief at his expression of pleasure was nearly palpable.

He raised a hand and the room stilled.

"However," he went on, the scowl returning to cool their enthusiasm, "all of that can be sabotaged by a mistake now. See to it that you do your duty properly, without question, and when that one world government comes about you will be lauded as saviors, heroes to be admired and rewarded for your sacrifice."

This time the applause was deafening.

Leaving the board room, he met his bodyguard in the private elevator to the lobby of the Enkeli Building, the 130-story headquarters of Andlat Enterprises in New York. Each of the three-man bodyguard had a wireless transceiver lodged in his right ear. A slight bulge under their coats at the left arm testified to the late model hand weapons they carried. The men were a few inches shorter than Azrael, but the sight of that company as it exited the elevator and stomped into the crowded lobby was enough to part the way without a word.

Waiting just outside, a black limousine idled. Azrael and his men climbed inside while police motorcycles took up positions before and behind as the motorcade moved off. Azrael was scheduled to address that tottering, senile figurehead of international brotherhood, the United Nations. He had to keep up his image, but secretly he relished the thought that the UN's days, like all the national representative organizations worldwide, were numbered.

They would soon be redundant.

2

The beast drew itself up, inhaling in readiness to unleash its hot breath at him. Maachen crouched behind the shield just in time, felt the heat of the dragon fire pour around him as he huddled in its shelter. Scorched earth smoked on both sides as it passed. He felt his armor's glow through the gambeson's padding, smelled the metal's temper.

He darted forward in the aftermath, squinting against the haze, to strike at the beast's exposed belly. He felt the blade penetrate, but only a few inches before the leviathan roared and spun away, nearly tearing the sword from his grip. He narrowly avoided the great spiked tail. Rolling to his right, he brought the shield up again to catch a blow from the tail as it returned, then slashed at it. The sword jarred ineffectually against hard scale.

* * *

"No?"

Nicholson shook his head again. He pushed an errant lock of dirty blond hair back. With his jaw set against Mason's suggestion, the angles of his face were exaggerated. "No," he repeated, firmly. "I barely escaped with my life last time. You want me to go back? Forget it."

The little front room was crowded with all of them gathered before the fireplace. Meeker was glad Mason had waited until after they had eaten to do this. She doubted she'd have had much appetite otherwise.

She chewed nervously on the inside of her cheek as she watched the exchange between Nicholson and Mason. Mason had explained the plan in detail, including the risks, leaving nothing to the imagination. The longer he spoke, the more alarmed she became. How could he ask Andrew to do this? There had to be a better way.

She looked at Stephen Overguard standing next to Mason. The big Texan stared at nothing, apparently not listening. She got the distinct impression he would have liked to have melted into the wall in spite of his tall frame. She knew he and Andrew didn't get along. Was he part of this already or was he hearing it for the first time, like the rest of them? Maybe he was staying quiet, not trusting himself to venture any opinion for fear she might think him jealous?

Jaelon and Malthusan leaned against the back wall, watching with impassive expressions. Jaelon fingered the little jeweled bull pendant hanging from her necklace. Malthusan's huge form was immobile, eyes half-closed, the rest of his face set in his perpetual scowl. Meeker doubted either of the Knights had an opinion about this. They spent most of their time away from Mason and the regulars, as if they were willing to participate only when they had to. Populus stood on the other side of Mason from Overguard, while John Tripp sat in the high-backed chair facing the fireplace, a glass of whiskey turning slowly in his hand. Tripp had already said he wanted out. Now that Andrew was part of the team, how much longer would he stay?

"I understand your concern," Mason started to say, moving over to the mantelpiece to prop his forearm atop it.

"My concern?" Nicholson scoffed. *"My concern?* Look, I've gone along with you and your people here because I had no choice. After I was shot in that bar, you took care of me, and I'm grateful. But time ran out on my options while I was recovering. That's why I agreed when you asked me to help. It was me who made it possible to bring down Catalina Industries. Don't you think Azrael will know who did that?"

Once again, the wards vibrated.

Populus stepped forward. "Yes, he will, but it won't matter."

"How do you know that for sure?" Nicholson shot back.

The Greek hesitated only a moment before answering, but even Meeker noticed it. She chewed her lower lip and glanced from one man to the other. Though they came from different times, outwardly they were very similar. In build, in stature, so very much the same, but in attitude...

"Minions pride themselves on their own skills in deception, Mr. Nicholson. Azrael's weakness is his confidence in his own deviousness. That very confidence will be his downfall," Populus insisted.

Meeker shivered at the wards' thrum. "Can we stop saying that name, please?"

"Look," Nicholson said, "you never worked for Az... for him. I did. I know the man, and I know what he's capable of." He shook his head again, and at that moment his gray eyes caught Meeker's.

She knew when he looked at her that he wanted her to speak up, to back him, but she was the newest member of the group, the youngest by far. She glanced at Mason, wondering if he would even consider her opinion.

She had always been a bit in awe of the Angelkiller – the way he took charge, always seemed to know exactly what to do, never lost confidence. The fact he was more than two thousand years old boggled her mind. She had never spoken to him in private. What would she say? How do you talk to someone who was alive before Europe was Europe?

"Never mind, Populus," Mason said, saving her from her confusion. "We'll have to find another..."

"I'll do it," Tripp said.

They turned to him. Tripp set the glass down on the side table by his chair. When he spoke, his New England accent betrayed his origins. Meeker couldn't help noticing how much older Tripp looked than when they'd first met.

"It doesn't matter," he went on, his brown eyes never leaving the fireplace. "I was done anyway. Believe me, I'd prefer to spend my remaining years on a little farm up north, but I guess we don't always get what we want in this life."

"John..."

Tripp held up his hand to stop Mason's objection. "Jonah, it's okay." He let out a long sigh. "It's really okay."

The company exchanged glances until Jaelon walked over

to Tripp and knelt down beside his chair. Tripp met her gaze when she placed her hand on his forearm.

"Your heart is in the right place, Mr. Tripp," she said, "but we cannot use you for this."

Tripp frowned. "Why not?"

"You were seen in the bar with us. The Minion would have reported that."

Tripp looked up at Nicholson, then back to Jaelon. "But, he was seen there, too."

Meeker realized at that moment just how disconnected Tripp had become. He had to have missed most of the conversation not to know Andrew was the only one who could carry out the mission with any chance of success. Clearly, the man was becoming more and more distant. Maybe it was a good thing he was retiring.

"The Enemy probably thinks Mr. Nicholson is dead," Jaelon explained.

Tripp looked more confused. Jaelon patiently repeated the plan, including Nicholson's part in it. Meeker admired the woman's gentle tone, her demeanor as if speaking to a child. Then it dawned on her that in Jaelon's eyes, Tripp probably was just that: a child needing care. The man listened without interjection until the Knight was finished, and Meeker suspected there was something more in her voice than just sympathy that soothed the man's confusion. In fact, Meeker found herself listening intently, as if hearing the story for the first time. It wasn't until the Knight stopped talking it dawned on her how odd that was.

"So you see, John," Mason put in, "we need to find another way to do this. One that won't put anyone in danger."

Tripp nodded thoughtfully, picked up his glass, and sipped it. He returned to contemplating the fireplace.

Mason looked at Tripp a few moments, his dark brow furrowed. Meeker could almost see his worry there. Those two men had been together for better than two hundred years. What must Mason be thinking, looking at Tripp's vacant stare?

The Angelkiller tore his gaze from Tripp and faced the others. "Suggestions?" he asked.

The room fell silent. When the quiet grew uncomfortable, Populus broke in.

"Since this was my idea, I suppose it's my responsibility to find an alternative," he said. "Give me some time to work."

Mason nodded. "Let us know if we can help. But, Populus, work quickly. I have the feeling things are proceeding faster than we know."

* * *

Nicholson's refusal shouldn't have surprised him.

Mason found himself secretly pleased. The man hadn't been with them long enough to be placed in that kind of position and, to be perfectly frank, Mason wasn't sure he trusted him that much anyway. He had only agreed to bring Nicholson in at the Knights' insistence. Their faith in the man had paid off in the demise of Catalina Industries, but Mason suspected there was a price yet to be paid for all that.

It wasn't the first time he'd been forced to work with untrustworthy allies and probably wouldn't be the last. The main thing he was concerned about was protecting the others from whatever consequences might arise. Past experience had taught him those consequences could be dire in the extreme.

Looking at Tripp's vacant face as his friend stared at the cold fireplace, he was reminded of a time long past, before he met the New Englander, before even he had been called to form this cell.

After his mentor died, he left the Celtiberian's stronghold in Gaul to wander the wilds of the Narbonensis and Cisalpina, years of following the southern beaches of the conquered territories along the Mediterranean. While Sorius lived, it was easy to take his word about the Great Conflict. His mentor was the kind of man one trusted and respected at first sight. Once the old man passed though, all the questions he had asked and thought answered forever resurfaced. The concept of good versus evil in the world was easy enough to understand, but the realization that evil had triumphed grated on him. He tramped from village to town to city, watching, contemplating what he saw, analyzing his conclusions, trying to use the tools Sorius gave him to ferret out Truth from appearance. For years, he busied himself with the mundane task of existence, working as a mercenary guard for wealthy merchants, a common laborer, even taking a try at being a tutor in military strategy for a rich Italian family. Wherever he went, he learned the languages and customs, and always he found evidence of the Conflict. His new-found ability to discern the signs of The Enemy showed him how deeply ingrained in the peoples' lives The Enemy's deception had become. As the years went by, he learned how to identify those controlled by Minions and to associate the otherwise pleasant aroma of lilac with them as they went about their nefarious activities.

The constant battering on his psyche eventually palled so badly on him he considered returning to the Holy Land and becoming a hermit, abandoning the seemingly pointless and unending, friendless struggle. He was at the point of booking passage on a grain ship bound for the port of Antioch when he got word of the discovery of the New World.

It was incredible news, a bit of hope in the darkness. He made his way back to Britain, unwilling to trust the Spanish and Portuguese with their intimate connections to the Moorish conquerors he fought against at Jerusalem and the bloody siege of Acre. His Roman roots kept him from wanting to cooperate with the descendants of his old enemies in Gaul and Iberia. It would be centuries before those memories would fade enough to let him forgive them, and himself, for what was done.

He took the name Jacomo Warder and joined a troop crossing the Atlantic late in the seventeenth century. The crossing was hard and dangerous. More than once it looked as if the ships would be lost forever in that bleak and unforgiving expanse where nothing lived above the surface but their tiny party of colonists and nothing but monsters with rows of serrated teeth lived below. Occasionally the glad sight of a pod of dolphin would entertain or the wondrous vision of a whale, larger than any he'd ever encountered, would lighten the voyagers' mood, but for the most part they fought their way westward, battling storm and disease and depression.

After what seemed years but was only a few months, the

survivors reached the Dover colony. The settlement was only a common building, a church, a few houses, a sawmill, and gristmill behind a wooden palisade, but to the new arrivals it was palatial, having been restricted to the decks for so long. Once they got their land legs back, the children ran wildly in the compound, their laughter a welcome balm to suffering spirits.

He found the New World both inspiring and troublesome. Contrary to popular reports, it wasn't uninhabited. Painted men in leather and feather wandered the forests outside the settlement. The residents were still in terror of the recent Indian raid that had claimed the life of their garrison commander, Major Richard Waldron. He soon found himself in the role of a captain, a front line defender. It was familiar and he fell into the position naturally.

He was happy for the first time in years.

But as time passed he knew he could not stay. His longevity was a problem that could not be hidden forever. Too soon, he had to fake his death during an Indian attack and head south toward the Massachusetts Colony where he was just another wandering soul looking for a home.

In Massachusetts, he got word of a disturbance that could only be the handiwork of a Minion. Drawn irresistibly by his sense of duty, he traveled to Roxbury and soon found himself attached to a witch hunter named Increase Goodman, whose company had accused a local woman of witchcraft. The woman, whom he recognized with surprise and alarm as the Minion itself, was terrorizing the farmers around Roxbury for no other reason than for its own amusement.

He had never actually faced a Minion before. In the old countries, he had fought against their agents and lieutenants, but the Minions themselves preferred to stay in the background rather than place themselves in danger. He tried his best to argue Goodman from facing it directly, but the man boldly faced it head on. His death was both agonizing and very public, making the general panic worse.

He knew he couldn't defeat the Minion by himself, and with the death of the witch hunter the rest of his company had disappeared into the surrounding countryside. Dismayed, he retreated to New York to consider. It was there he met Jonathan Prester of Saybrook.

There was an immediate connection between them, as if they had known each other all their lives. Mason found himself opening up to the man about his life and beliefs in a way he had never imagined possible. Prester and he spent long hours discussing faith, religion, and politics. In a very short time, they became fast friends, so Mason was not surprised when Prester offered to use his considerable financial resources against the Minion. Although Prester was not yet aware of the true nature of The Enemy, Mason knew he'd found a kindred spirit. Here was someone who was unafraid to confront evil at its source.

Prester hired a small army of militiamen, firing their zeal with an oratorical skill Mason hadn't heard since the days before the march on Jerusalem, when Godfrey of Bouillon had inspired his troops to fight and die. Listening to Prester, he was reminded of his own promise to Sorius: to resist The Enemy whenever and wherever it might be found.

He discovered the strength to be what he'd long forgotten he was: a soldier in the Master's service.

The confrontation with that Minion resulted in three things. First, the Minion was overwhelmed and banished, but the militia was killed to the last man. Mason and Prester survived, wounded and spent, to pass their recovery in the Minion's burnt out dwelling. Second, the experience cemented their friendship, which extended to the present day. And last, it showed him he could depend on another in the fight, giving him the confidence to build on that trust and eventually become the head of a group whose members would resist The Enemy for years to come.

Prester took the name John Tripp and he began calling

himself Jonah Mason when they left the colonies shortly after the Revolutionary War. The fallout from the Minion's death left a power vacuum in The Enemy's ranks, preventing retaliation while they bickered amongst themselves and covering their departure.

They reached the western frontier, always just ahead of the developing states, living at the edge of civilization as trappers, hunters, guides, and scouts. They appointed themselves lookouts for Enemy influences that threatened to establish themselves on the periphery of the growing nation.

He wondered how it was he had lived all these years next to The Enemy yet had personally remained untouched by that influence. He looked at the Knights, all of whom where younger than he, and wondered how they had found their way into such an exalted status while he remained little more than a front line soldier in the Conflict.

Had he been found wanting for so long? What prevented him from being their equal? What had he done, or what had he neglected doing, that kept him from their ranks?

A profound ache resounded within him, a pain he realized that, until now, he had refused to acknowledge. Tears, long a stranger to him, rose unbidden, and he turned his face from the others, suddenly ashamed but not knowing why.

The duties of leadership had demanded so much of his attention for so long, he hadn't taken time to examine his own motives. Was it because of the Knights' presence that only now he began to question himself? Those tears, bitter and unexpected, were they for himself or for those he'd known and lost? Had grief and regret finally found him?

Hadn't he done enough? What more did the Master want from him?

An unreasoning anger threatened to overwhelm him as a parade of faces flashed in his memory. All the lives he'd seen destroyed by The Enemy haunted him, all the chances he'd missed to speak out against iniquity and injustice assailed his conscience. With an effort, he held back from crying out in frustration. He was just one man, after all. What could he do against the enormity of what he'd seen? Thousands of years, thousands of lives, pressed down on him, the weight of it all so much to bear.

He slowly made his way to the chair by Tripp and sank heavily into it, welcoming the comfort of its support for his sudden weakness. He wiped his eyes and sighed.

"Jonah?" he heard Tripp say. His friend gazed at him, puzzled. "Something wrong?"

He shook his head. "No."

Tripp looked at him for another moment. "Wanna talk?"

He glanced around and found Jaelon watching him.

"It's nothing," he told Tripp. "Just thinking."

Jaelon looked for a moment as if she might approach and he found he didn't want that, looked away. Did she sense what he was thinking? He knew she might, that her intuition was strong, that she might possibly feel his distress. They were alike in many ways. The Knights knew loss and possibly even shared his regrets. Having lived so long, how could they not?

He envied her calm, but was that no more than a front? Was it nothing more than a facade built to hid her own inner turmoil? He wished he could know her thoughts, but like everyone else he was alone inside his head, a prisoner of his past, a slave to his present.

He smiled grimly. He was getting old, not just in years. Life was getting the better of him. He picked up a book and tried to lose himself in its pages, looking for escape from his past, comfort for the present.

* * *

Jaelon watched Mason as he stood, silently staring into space. It would soon enough be time to press him for his final decision about the choice given him. As the leader of this cell, he worked in a limited way for the cause. As a Knight, he could do so much more, but the sacrifice involved... Was that what was bothering him? It looked to her as if there was more than that. She recognized the signs of deep emotional stress, had felt that herself before her Vision came to allay those feelings. He sat by Tripp and for a moment their eyes met. She wanted to reach out to him, offer him reassurance, but the connection was gone almost as soon as it was made. He turned away too quickly, telling her he was not yet ready. She would not rush him. The decision must be from his heart, of his own free will. There was no other way.

The waiting was wearing on them all. She knew they all preferred action to this interminable stasis. It gave no comfort that this was part of the Conflict, these interludes of preparation, staging, and timing. All conflicts consist of long periods of boredom interspersed with minutes of terror and combat, whether physical or not. Still, she preferred action, with its inevitable conclusion of victory or defeat, to this frustration.

The time between conflicts was ever filled with memory. She pitied Mason most in these times. His memories must be hardest to endure of all his people. The others, simply by the fact of being younger, would have less to weigh down their conscience. Perhaps the person best equipped to handle this hiatus was Tripp. His fixation on the Seraph gave him a focal point for his attention, did not allow him to page through the catalog of the past. She noticed his glass was empty again, ignored as he stared into the fireplace.

Tripp must be allowed to leave before this came to a head. In his current condition, he would be a danger to himself and possibly to everyone else.

* * *

Seraph.

The word still rang in his head. Tripp sat very still and let the image spin in his mind's eye. Just the sight of it, that momentary glimpse, struck him to his core. It was beautiful and terrible at once, a mind-wrenching paradox of fright and yearning, awesome yet familiar. The vision haunted him waking and sleeping, not that he would want it to stop. Its presence was as much a comfort as it was uncomfortable. He pushed away the unpleasantness with all his might and clung to the joy. And what unutterable joy it was! Remembering the Seraph was a roller coaster of emotions, a constant shifting between wonder at its beauty and the awareness of his own failing before its perfection. Still, he would not want the memory erased for all the pain it evoked.

Minions were angels, he knew, dark angels in the service of The Enemy. He had faced them before, but how different was the memory of the Seraph from the thought of Minions.

He was reminded of that time in the Nevada territory. It seemed so long ago now, more of a dream or a nightmare, than reality.

He and Mason had been scouting ahead of a troop of US cavalry in what eventually would become Nevada. The desolate beauty of the scrub land and Joshua trees, the heat of the day and the chill of the bright nights, the surprising plethora of insects and reptiles, all appealed to his sense of order. He had happily ridden ahead of Mason one day, eager to see what lie over the next rise, when they came upon the Spanish mission.

It had been all but abandoned in the face of attacks by local Indians. Usually peaceful, the Moapa Paiute tribe had been whipped into a fury by a warrior named Red Lizard. This man came back changed from his vision quest, the ceremony reserved for communion with the gods. Where before the title of warrior extended mostly to hunting and the occasional skirmish with outlying tribes, Red Lizard was now a wild-eyed, bloodthirsty fighter with a special hatred for the Franciscan monks, blaming them for the recent raids by slave traders. By the time Tripp and Mason arrived, most of the missionaries had fled or been killed. Only the abbot remained, determined to face Red Lizard to the last, buttressed by his faith.

Tripp met a couple of the Moapa out hunting. He and Mason had adopted the dress of French fur traders for convenience to deal with natives, just a light leather jerkin and breeches under a beaver coat. The French seldom got this far west, but when they did, the natives never saw them as a threat and traded freely with them.

The Indians warned him about the feud between Red Lizard and the mission, using a broken form of Spanish they probably picked up from the missionaries. After a bit of effort, he was able to piece together the details of the conflict. The natives even told him to stay away from the mission because Red Lizard himself would be going there to kill the last of the Spanish in the next few days.

He carried the news back to Mason at camp. It wasn't a stretch to imagine Red Lizard had communed with something sinister on his vision quest. They decided to investigate further.

The mission turned out to be the burned out hulk of a church lying in the middle of several charred ruins arranged in a vague rectangle. The thatched roofs were gone, what remained of them just smoking heaps of ash behind the shattered adobe walls. The mission bells lay cracked and crushed in the patio.

Rust-colored stains in the dried mud walls gave witness to recent violence. Fresh crosses stood over three rows of eight graves, none of which looked to be more than a year old. They tied their horses to the post outside the church and walked in.

The abbot appeared almost at once, an elderly man in a clean black habit that stood out against his gray hair and haggard expression. One look at him told Tripp the man had come to accept his fate more as penance for the loss of his flock than anything else. The man's face was a study in grief and remorse. For all that, he greeted them and offered to share his water and what little food he had left. The mission gardens and fields had been burned and its herds dispersed so he wasn't able to offer much, but what he had he offered without reservation. Tripp and Mason politely refused and brought several days rations from their own stock to supplement the abbot's meager larder.

They stayed over the old man's objections. The abbot shook his head at what he considered their foolhardiness as they primed their weapons and took up positions to defend him, ignoring his pleas to leave.

It was several days before Red Lizard appeared. When he did, he didn't come alone. Six warriors swept into the ruined mission with him, howling and whooping, pausing only at the sound of Mason's flintlock pistol. He leveled his other pistol at them, dropped the spent weapon, and pulled yet another from his belt.

Tripp, concealed behind the broken line of a nearby wall, watched as Red Lizard and Mason stared silently at each other. The Indian was large, a formidable presence even standing still. He was dressed only in a hide loincloth, the rest of his body covered with garish tattoos and variously colored designs in war paint. His head was bald except for a short mane that began at his crown and went down to his neck. It was held together with thin leather straps, bloody beads their only ornamentation. The other warriors, dressed in similar fashion, stood uncertain. Red Lizard was their leader, the one reason they'd forsaken their peaceful life for this raiding and killing. That he should hesitate at anything was troubling.

The silent contest of wills stretched into more than a minute. Finally, Red Lizard grinned. He dropped his weapons and invited Mason to do the same, motioning him forward. Mason slowly stripped off his powder horn and ammunition pouch, warily eyeing Red Lizard and the others. The Indian saw his reluctance and waved his warriors back with a barked command. The six men moved off. Tripp thought he saw relief in their faces.

Mason placed his loaded pistols on the ground and

held out his hands to indicate he was unarmed. Red Lizard reached behind him and produced a *wi'hi,* a long blade used for skinning and gutting game. This he tossed at Mason's feet. Contemptuously, he motioned Mason to pick it up. Mason kicked it aside and shook his head. Red Lizard grinned more widely.

The Indian charged, roaring.

Mason stepped aside at the last second, delivering a sweeping kick that knocked Red Lizard heavily to the ground. Tripp clearly heard a snap as the Indian hit. Red Lizard staggered to his feet, his left arm hanging loosely. He glared at Mason, then calmly grabbed his elbow with his right hand and yanked. There was a grisly crunch. Red Lizard winced a little, then flexed his arm and hand.

Tripp tore his gaze from the fight to check the other warriors. They stood awestruck as the combat continued. Obviously, no one had challenged Red Lizard before and lived. He heard one of them say something in a low, furtive tone that sounded like *maru tawachi iyevupuni* before two of them slipped away quietly. From what little Paiute he understood, Tripp doubted they would be a threat. He went back to watching the fight.

Red Lizard and Mason were circling each other now, looking for an opening, gauging strength. Neither man seemed anxious to make the first move, and Tripp thought that perhaps it had gone as far as it was going to. Then, Red Lizard charged again.

Mason didn't step aside this time, instead charging in turn. They crashed together and locked arms around each other, trying to throw their opponent. Whoever won the wrestling contest would come out with the upper hand, possibly winning the fight outright. He'd seen these bouts before at different Indian camps. They were seldom to the death. It was encouraging to believe that perhaps Red Lizard had accepted Mason as the mission champion and would honor that the victor would dictate the fate of the settlement.

After a few minutes he could see the men were well-matched in strength and agility. They grappled back and forth across the plaza, stirring up dust and ash, kicking debris and nearly falling over the remains of a broken water trough. Neither man uttered anything other than the occasional grunt, but their expressions spoke volumes.

Red Lizard was tiring. Even Tripp could see that. Mason's military training and long experience with hand-to-hand combat was beginning to tell.

Of a sudden, the Indian lost his footing and went down.

"Ca'ikai!" Red Lizard said, holding his hand out

defensively. He grimaced and clutched his side. "U maupa."

Mason stepped back, panting, and leaned against the wall of the church. Both men were plainly exhausted. Tripp was amazed they could move at all.

It was only then Tripp realized Red Lizard had a reason for falling at that particular spot. The *wi'hi* was only an arm's length away, where Mason had kicked it. In a flash, the Indian snatched it, bolted up, and went for Mason. Surprised, Mason only had time to raise an arm to defend himself.

Tripp brought his rifle to bear and squeezed the trigger as Red Lizard's knife struck. The ammo ball hit the Indian hard enough to knock him clear of Mason, who clutched a gash on his forearm. Red Lizard stirred once, tried to rise, then collapsed and didn't move. Tripp dropped the rifle and turned to confront the other warriors, grabbing for his pistols.

All he saw were their retreating backs as they disappeared into the surrounding scrub. Behind him, there was a rushing noise, as of an approaching storm. He turned.

The Indian's body shuddered heavily, darkened until the skin and loincloth were blacker than a night sky. The tattoos glowed strange colors as a mist seeped from them to rise and coalesce above the corpse into a vaguely humanoid shape. The form lost its external limbs, becoming merely a torso and head, then the upper portion swelled until there was nothing but a hideous and demonic visage hovering above the body. Tripp felt a growing terror, looking at that apparition. He wanted to look away, but was suddenly afraid if he did it would attack him, take from him more than just his life.

The face glared at Mason from burning eyes alive with hate and malice, then its mouth stretched wide and it flew toward the man as if to devour him. Mason ducked as the smoky vision passed over him to dissipate into the air.

Red Lizard's body disappeared during the night. They assumed his tribesmen took it back to their camp. It was too unsettling to think of anything other than that.

He sipped at the glass, realized it was empty and wondered how long it had been that way. He placed it carefully on the little end table and gazed at its transparency. Deep within that emptiness he could almost see the Seraph's afterimage, a shadow made of light limned in a shimmer of iridescence. Not for the first time he wished he had the words for the colors within that glimmer. If he could just describe it, perhaps he could recover that profound shock of feelings, the overwhelming flood of conflicting emotions, the deep awareness of eternity that evaded complete recall because of the inadequacy of his comprehension of what he saw.

* * *

Nicholson glowered at Mason, huddled over a book as if nothing had happened.

What had he been thinking? How could he have talked himself into cooperating with these people? So what if they had pulled him out of the bar and looked after him? They'd only done it for their own purposes, not out of concern for him. As soon as he was well, they'd conned him into working for them to destroy his own company. They told him it was Azrael who'd tried to have him killed, but how did he know that for sure? All he had was their word for it. Everything they told him about the person who shot him could have been a lie manufactured from information stolen when they hacked his company files.

How much did he really know about these people anyway? Only what he'd seen since his recovery; only what they'd allowed him to know. They might as well still be as many ghosts to him now as they had always been in spite of the fact he had been with them so long.

True, they had some impressive tech and obviously were part of a larger, powerful organization. But they could just be some global corporate espionage arm of a competitor to Andlat Enterprises. This story about a Great Conflict? This eternal enmity between them and an ancient Enemy? How had he allowed himself to believe such hogwash? It was obviously nothing more than an elaborate, fantastic charade for his benefit. The more he mulled the situation, the more convinced he became he had been played. Their secretiveness, their scheming plans, their constant watchfulness, all convinced him more with each passing hour that they were not to be trusted.

Especially Mason.

The man was an enigma. The others deferred to his leadership with varying degrees of compliance. At times it was hard to know if he or Jaelon was truly in charge. It was as if they were actually two units, each with their own agenda, working together out of convenience.

Or were they really unaware of the others' agenda and actually working at odds?

Whatever the truth might be, he didn't intend to get caught in between when it finally panned out. He had to get out from under.

Maybe he could find his own way back. He still had contacts on the outside, people who owed him. Maybe it was time to call in some markers, cash in on those backup plans he had put in place. No businessman worth his salt burned all his bridges. He still had a few aces to play.

But how to get out without these people hounding him? That was the question. They had shown themselves more than capable of being formidable enemies. They weren't likely to just let him walk away, not with all he knew now. He needed leverage.

As he considered the situation, Meeker walked by, headed toward the kitchen.

There was the girl and she already looked interested in him. Could he use that attraction? He could tell she was the least experienced of the group, an obvious neophyte to whatever this group's true organization might be. The others treated her comparatively gently. They would be very protective of her, making her the perfect hostage should things go sour.

Of course, she must be handled with care until he made his move. No sense in making things difficult. Ideally, she would come away of her own accord. They certainly wouldn't object to that.

He set out to follow her.

3

The Persian Empire troops that were gathered on the European Bloc's border now numbered more than half a million. Their equipment ranged from decades-old armored vehicles to state-of-the-art robotic surveillance drones. Imperial satellites hurtled overhead, mapping the opponent's defenses. The European nations, even those who previously signed treaties with the Empire, watched anxiously as the flag of the Caliph rose over buildings previously used by Slavic governments, now Imperial puppets.

Populus wondered how long it might be before the dam broke. Imperial troops hovered ready, but something held them in check yet. Was it The Enemy himself? Could it be that the other cells were having success in their own missions? Being a cog in a larger machine often was frustrating. He wished he knew the whole of the bigger picture. Then again, would that make what he had to do any easier? Some of Mason's cell would not survive the coming storm, that much was certain. If he knew the whole of the Master's plan, could he go through with it?

Best to concentrate on what he could do rather than speculate on what he might. He turned his attention to finding an answer to their latest problem. Where could they set up that The Enemy would least expect and be least likely to look?

He leaned over the computer and started to work.

* * *

Stephen Overguard sat on the little front porch, thinking. He knew he shouldn't be doing it, but the only thing he could think about was Janice and Nicholson.

He put his face in his hands and grit his teeth. Maybe it was a mistake to bring Janice into the cell. Ever since she joined, the nagging concern for her safety had stood uppermost in his thoughts. The massacre at Vera Cruz played over and over in his mind, the deaths of so many of his cell in Mexico a recurrent horror that refused to die. The lone survivor, he had been plagued by guilt for years afterward, still felt a pang when he thought of it.

Now, the nightmares that haunted him for so long

afterward had come back, robbing him of much needed rest. Too often in those nightmares one of the bodies he'd found twisted and mangled now looked like Janice. He'd thought being reassigned might help, take him away from the brooding on the past and let him focus on the future. Janice had come along and that future began to look better.

Then Nicholson came.

He couldn't help but see Janice was attracted to the man. Not that you could blame her. He was attractive in a snobbish, metrosexual kind of way. How could he, a Texas boy, compete with that? Nicholson was the kind of man you found in fashion videos – soft and slick. He probably hadn't done an honest day's work in his life. The man reminded him of a snake, with Janice the helpless bird hypnotized by its gaze.

Overguard leaned back on the porch and looked up at the unbroken sky. Why couldn't things be simple any more? When he had first joined the Army after the fall of Israel, he had been full of enthusiasm, motivated to do his best against The Enemy. Back then, it was easy to know who was for and against you. Now, with Mason making a deal with Azrael and recruiting Nicholson, it just didn't seem so clear-cut.

But what could he do about it? Mason was their leader, had been for years. He had never questioned that. Neither had any of the cell. Even Chandler had trusted Mason without reserve.

Maybe he shouldn't have. Chandler became the first of their cell to fall casualty to The Enemy. Then, Martin.

Come to think of it, how had Mason survived for so long? How had the man avoided the fate of most Army members? Could it be that this latest deal made with Azrael was just one of many? Could it be that Mason stayed alive because he played both sides?

Overguard sat stunned at the thought. What did he know about Mason, really? Central had assigned him to Mason after the Vera Cruz incident. He wanted some time away to put his thoughts in order, but Central had insisted that he should stay active. Even so, it took the Vatican bombing to convince him to sign on with Mason. It seemed the right thing to do. Now...

Had he been assigned to Mason for another, more covert reason? And why did not one but *three* Knights suddenly appear just when Mason made his deal?

He stood up and squared his jaw. Whatever the truth might be, he had not forgotten his purpose. He was willing to protect his cell against all comers.

No matter who they might be.

* * *

Antonio Malthusan chewed on the remains of a toothpick and considered Mason's plan. He had to admit the majority of it went over his head. All this about computers had never been interesting to him. Give him a fine weapon, a target, and time to prepare. That was all he needed. Everyone made life so complex, but it had never been that way. Life was simply survival. You were loyal to your Master and used all your strength in His service. That was enough, should be enough for anyone.

He liked Mason. The man had strength. The others respected him. He was a leader. Malthusan knew leaders when he saw them. As a soldier, he had served under many, good and bad. He'd watched men used like cattle for the sake of a few feet of territory, and at other times seen commanders on the front lines rallying men on the brink of surrender. He hadn't been with Mason long enough to make a real judgment as to which side of that line the man came down on, but he was leaning toward the better side.

Jaelon walked by him as she paced the floor. Waiting was always the hardest part of an operation, and Jaelon paced when she waited. He figured it had to be a byproduct of her time as a slave, manacled and caged. He watched her for several minutes, admiring her movements. Her dark hair gathered together at the shoulder with leather straps, her cat-like grace, her skin darkened by Mediterranean sun almost obscuring the faded evidence of Pictish tattoos... She was the main reason he had agreed to stay on with her and Populus after Clement's death.

He had no illusions about his feelings for Jaelon, and knew she was aware of them. He was content to be around her. He knew there could be nothing more than that between them, and long ago came to accept that fact. In the old days, perhaps he wouldn't have been so at ease with that. The centuries had dampened the fires of his temper. He was less the reckless mercenary of his youth and more the deliberate soldier the Army needed.

Jaelon was allowing Mason to make decisions for them. There was a time he wouldn't have stood for that, back when gold meant everything to him. He had always prided himself in being his own man. Sure, he had his price then, but that was just business. Services rendered. If a better deal came along, he'd take it without hesitation. You survived by being loyal only to yourself in those days. He'd learned that only too well when the "Romans" came and burned his village.

They may have been a motley crew of mercenaries themselves, dressed in the remains of Roman grandeur, but their *gladii* were sharp enough. They raided his settlement on the east coast of Cyprus, burned their boats, stole their stores and took slaves. Malthusan, a mere boy at the time, found he was small enough to hide in the rocks nearby.

Huddled in the cold and damp, terrified of discovery at every noise, he cried himself to sleep at last. The bellowing laughter of the raiders as they entertained themselves in unspeakable ways on the surviving villagers echoed in his ears. The noise of the surf finally won out over their revelry and the wan starlight soon shone through as the smoke from the burning village was swept away by the sea breeze.

For two more days he hid, slaking his thirst on the dew glistening from the rocks at sunrise. Hunger at last drove him from hiding and he timidly returned home. He never forgot what he found there. It would haunt him all his days.

Only the sound of the sea trying in vain to wash away the broken skeletons of the fishing boats broke the heavy silence hanging over the charred scene. Most of the thatched huts were reduced to smoldering shells. The dead lay everywhere in various states of dismemberment and decomposition, some imprisoned in torn and tangled nets.

He picked his way through the ruins, scraping for any bit of bread or dried fish the raiders might have missed. It took most of the morning, but he finally found enough to sate his appetite and a little more.

As the day went on, others arrived who had fled as he did, mostly children his age. They fought for the scraps. He usually won.

His greatest find was a slightly bent *gladius*, looted from one of the few dead raiders. He'd never held a sword before, but the weight of it as he closed his fist around its hilt was comforting. The way the others shied from him as he lifted it filled him with a sensation of power. After that, no one vied with him for his food.

From that day, he became an extension of the sword.

He learned to fight, to steal, even kill when necessary. He stayed within a few days distance of the destroyed village for some time, hoping for and dreading the raiders' return. A part of him wanted vengeance for his loss, but a more practical part of him knew it would never happen. At last, he moved inland toward the capital of Nicosia, where there was easy food and a chance to find shelter better than the makeshift hovels he could manage alone. On his way he stole food from the fields and hid from irate farmers. He avoided the wagon tracks and hunting trails. The raid haunted his dreams and gave him a terror of strangers. When the walls of Nicosia rose before him he hesitated, fighting that part of himself that balked at the thought of crowded streets and plazas. The stench of the city – sweat, manure, urine, smoke, rot – didn't help. He thought of the breath of the sea, its salty taste on the tongue, the fresh touch of an ocean zephyr. It was several days before he could gather the strength to walk through the city gates.

Getting into Nicosia was easy. Staying alive inside proved harder than he expected. More than once he was glad of his sword. Dealing with thieves, beggars, and cutthroats became a regular part of life as he grew in stature, strength, and reputation. By his twentieth summer he was head of his own troop, a minor dignitary in Nicosia's underworld.

The major drawback to having a high profile was it made him a better target for the ambitious. Eventually, even the well-connected political forces began to eye his growing influence with a jaundiced eye.

When he fled the raiders the second time, they were unarmed, dressed in fine brocades and filigreed costumes. He barely escaped with his life, managing by luck to carry off a third of what he had accrued, but spending a good deal of it to buy passage to the mainland on a grain ship bound for Athens. He had no fear of starting over, so his arrival in a foreign land merely provided new targets to acquire and control.

That is, until the Ottoman Turks came. Then everything changed.

"Antonio?"

Malthusan snapped back to the present. Jaelon peered at him with concern on her face.

"Are you well?" she asked.

"Yes," he grunted. He tasted wood, realized he'd chewed the toothpick to bits. "Pardon," he mumbled, and strode out the door to spit the pulp on the ground by the porch, nearly hitting Overguard in the process.

"Hey!" the Texan yelped. "Watch it!"

Malthusan picked pulp off his tongue and spit again. He gave Overguard an appraising look. The man was large, with a morose quality Malthusan disliked and became more pronounced each day. He wasn't sure what to make of that. He wondered if anyone else noticed. There was an air of death around the man, as if he carried a curse. How was that possible? Surely the Master would not allow such a thing?

A light touch on his shoulder brought him around.

"You are sure you are well?" Jaelon asked again.

"I am," he said, nodding.

Her hand lingered another moment, then was gone. The warmth of her touch remained briefly, was gone too soon.

"Very well, then," she said, frowning.

She slowly turned and went back inside. Overguard followed her, glaring at him as he went by.

4

The reports from the Eastern Bloc were disheartening enough, but the news of floods of refugees into the European Bloc from the occupied Slavic states, of the horrors compounded on a terrified, starving wave of humanity deeply appalled Populus.

In his early days, he'd seen gross violence and hideous deeds, but never on this scale. The iron fist of Rome, the collar of the Byzantines, the dehumanization of entire populations under the Ottoman Caliphs, even the horrors of the twentieth century's death camps paled in comparison to the scope of this exodus. Whole cities surged westward against the Persian juggernaut, reminding him of that army whose advance so long ago looked unstoppable.

"Was a Thermopylae even possible in this day and age?" he wondered. "And if so, whose sacrifice would be required to win it?"

He looked up from his workstation at the others. Tripp had not moved from his chair, still watching the dark fireplace. It was obvious to him, if to no one else, that Tripp was already gone from them, lost in his memory of what he had seen in the park, was it just a few days ago? How much had changed in such a short time! Populus marveled at the velocity of events since their arrival.

Mason sat in the other chair in front of the fireplace, to all appearances reading a book. Populus couldn't make out the title, but he doubted it made a difference. Like himself, Mason had learned the art of waiting, an art that took centuries to learn and millennia to master. It required finding a quiet within oneself that even the anticipation of a tomorrow could not spoil. It was the result of the acceptance of the moment as it came, without thought for the possibilities of the future or regret for missed chances in the past.

Jaelon, as was her wont, paced. She stopped suddenly and spoke to Malthusan in a low voice, then followed him outside.

"Any luck?"

He looked up to find Meeker standing beside him. She did tend to hover when she was worried.

"Still working," he replied. "Tell me, my dear, what do you think?"

She blinked at him. "About what?"

"Our plan."

The girl paused before answering. He could tell she was considering her answer carefully and guessed she disapproved. Her apparent attraction to Nicholson no doubt contributed to that. In his own experience, affairs of the heart needlessly complicated things, but that was a lesson he'd learned long ago.

Looking into her youthful, open face carried him back to his own earlier days. He felt a twist in his chest at the memory. Strange. No matter how much time intervened, the thought of home always brought back the vision of a quiet villa amidst an olive grove. He could still see the δουλικός, the household servants, as they went about their work, picking, sorting, carrying the ripe fruit...

"Frankly, I don't like it," Meeker said, breaking him from his thoughts. "I think it's reckless and dangerous and I don't understand how you and Mason could present it in the first place."

He nodded slowly. "I see," he said, then turned back to his workstation. "Well, you need not worry yourself further, my dear. It seems we must find another way."

"Good!" she barked.

He looked over his shoulder at her. Was she that upset?

Could her attraction to Nicholson be deeper than suspected?

She wilted under his gaze and walked off. Populus frowned. He had seen the relationship between the girl and Overguard. The group could ill afford the drama of a love triangle right now, not with the prospect of real progress against Azrael in the offing. He wondered if he should speak to the girl about that. No, best let Jaelon do it. He doubted the girl would be enchanted with the idea of an old man prying into her private affairs. Yes, best talk to Jaelon about it, and soon.

* * *

Overguard shook off his annoyance at Malthusan. He needed to talk to one of the Knights, but not him. He was just the muscle. If he was going to talk to anyone, it would have to be Jaelon or Populus. Jaelon had walked back into the cabin ahead of him, but when he tried to get her attention she ignored him. He thought about shouting to get her attention, but reconsidered when he saw Janice walking away from Populus. The Greek watched her step away, then caught Overguard looking at him. He squared his shoulders and approached the Greek.

"Why are you here?" Overguard asked bluntly.

"Pardon?"

"You and the other two. Why are you here?"

Populus looked taken aback. He was plainly confused.

"We were sent to help," he told Overguard.

The big Texan loomed over him, his bulk suddenly intimidating. Populus had to lean back to face him.

"If there was just one of ya, I would buy that. Not three," Overguard rumbled, his drawl becoming more pronounced as his face reddened. "Why? Tell me, why?"

"Honestly, to help."

Overguard leaned in closer. "You're here for Mason, ain't ya?"

Populus pulled a little farther away.

"Why didn't you take him before Martin disappeared?"

"Mr. Overguard, I assure you..."

"I don't know what yer game is," Overguard interrupted, "but I'll find out. I won't let you or Mason sacrifice anyone else."

"I..."

Overguard wasn't listening. He was walking away.

* * *

Populus watched Overguard move into the front room. The man's attitude was most unexpected. An argument, even physical conflict between Overguard and Nicholson would have been more likely to him. Where had this sudden paranoia come from?

He rose and found Jaelon in the little kitchen pouring herself a glass of water. She sipped it as he spoke.

"I have just had a most disturbing conversation with Mister Overguard."

"About Meeker?"

"About Mason and us."

"Indeed?" She set the empty glass on the counter.

"He seems to think we have a sinister agenda."

"What exactly did he say?"

Populus briefly recapped the conversation. Jaelon listened in silence until he finished.

"So, he did not accuse us of anything," she observed.

"Not outright," he allowed.

She nodded, considering. Populus leaned against the counter.

"What should we do?" he asked.

"I do not see anything we can do but have faith the Master will manage it."

He looked away as she washed her glass. She was right, of course. They could take no action against Overguard unless the man turned on them. Still, he had a bad feeling, perhaps a premonition.

* * *

Meeker was furious and embarrassed, mortified at her reaction. The man had asked a simple question, so why had she jumped down his throat? What came over her? What must he think?

The door opened and Jaelon and Overguard came in. Jaelon looked worried. Stephen looked annoyed. She wondered what they'd been talking about out there. Stephen had become increasingly distant since Andrew joined them. She suspected his jealousy was deeper than he let on, but how could she convince him that her attraction to Andrew was not serious? Andrew was different from Stephen in so many ways, ways that fascinated her but didn't really mean much otherwise.

Men were so difficult to understand.

"Something wrong?"

She almost jumped at Nicholson's voice behind her.

"Not really," she said with a sheepish smile. "I was just talking to Populus."

"Yeah, he seems to be having an odd effect on everyone today. Say, are you up for a walk? It's a bit close in here for me right now."

"Well..." She glanced around, looking for Stephen.

She found him in low conversation with Populus, who was scowling deeply. Something was bothering them, that much she could see. That meant another meeting, more planning, more scheming. Frankly, she was sick of that for now. "Yes," she told Nicholson, "I think a walk would be just the thing."

He offered his arm in an exaggerated gesture. "Madam?"

She slipped her hand into the crook of his elbow and smiled.

* * *

Mason found the Greek sitting before his computer, frowning at the screen though he seemed to be staring vacantly, as if preoccupied with something else.

"How are things going? Any progress?" he asked.

The Knight shook himself and motioned him to approach.

"Indeed there is. I think I may have found a solution to our problem," Populus told him. "There are abandoned airbases near most of the megaplexes," He indicated several locations on the screen. "The nearest to the Memphisplex is only about 30 miles northwest of the perimeter."

"Is it totally abandoned?" Mason asked, peering at the screen.

"The government never completely abandons anything,"

Populus told him. "Especially in the case of old airbases. There is always the possibility it could be used in future, so they maintain a security detail, albeit a small one."

"What do we know about that?"

The Knight tapped on the computer and handed Mason an I/O set.

"It's easier to show you than describe it."

Mason slipped the set around his neck and pressed it against his flesh. He ignored the initial disorientation and waited for Populus to boot.

He was flying over a virtual rendition of the Memphisplex environs, probably a pirated satellite linkup. The sprawling megaplex straddled the ancient banks of the Mississippi River, stretching for miles either side. Its perimeter formed a perfect circle beyond which few besides some law enforcement personnel traveled. Within that border a civilization burgeoned nearly self-sufficient, one of hundreds spread across North America, echoed all over the world. People were born, grew, lived, and died inside those walls, never seeing anyplace outside, never realizing their isolation, educated only in their immediate surroundings.

For the majority of people, not just in the Memphisplex but in every complex, their population constituted all of humanity.

There were no others. Nor did they think that odd, since most had lived within the confines of the megaplex for years, some for their entire lives. Over the last few decades, The Enemy had made great strides toward this balkanization of mankind. It was easier to control pods of small populations than manage a global society. By separating people into communities independent of each other, The Enemy had found a way to make it more difficult to involve people in concern for their neighbor's welfare. They had tried at first to divide humanity through political and religious factions, but even with centuries of experience they were unable to completely alienate the feelings of compassion and charity toward others. It wasn't until The Enemy struck on this physical isolation, selling it under the guise of security and sufficiency, that they made significant strides toward success. The major factor in accomplishing that goal was the interweb, which gave each person the illusion of a personal connection with the outside world. Such connections were, of course, strictly controlled, monitored, and filtered by large corporations such as Andlat Enterprises.

The edge of the Memphisplex passed under him, revealing less detail as he flew farther along. Here there was an indication of an old roadbed, probably the remains of the interstate system. There, the imprint of what might have once been tilled farmland gone back to nature. Once in a while he saw broken hulks of neglected fueling stations long the roadbed, accompanied by the odd erection standing close by with a collapsed roof, possibly an abandoned store or restaurant.

At last the image sharpened again, indicating he was approaching the area of the old airbase. It was small, with a single runway and taxiway alongside a few standing structures. Of the most concern was the sight of a heloship parked near the largest edifice. Support vehicles shuttled back and forth from it to the building.

The heloship might or might not be armed. It was unlikely it would be, as it was probably used for patrolling the outer perimeter of the megaplex, looking for animal incursions or needed maintenance. It lacked military or law enforcement markings, which was encouraging, but was undoubtedly connected into the local communications networks. A single transmission from it would bring the full fury of The Enemy on them in minutes.

Mason took several minutes to scrutinize the landscape around the airbase for cover. If they were going to take the base, they needed to know how to get to it safely, which buildings needed to be captured, and what was necessary to hold it. The more he scanned the picture, the more convinced he became the mission would be impractical.

He pulled the I/O off and shook his head.

"It's no good," he told Populus. "There's no way we can get into the base without being discovered. Even if we could, how would we hold it once the takeover was found out? It's indefensible with the limited resources we have."

"You misunderstand," the Greek said. "I was not proposing we capture the base. I was proposing we use its communications infrastructure to access what we need."

"Ah," Mason said, fingering the I/O set. "How close do we need to get to the base to do that?"

Populus scratched his chin for a moment. "No farther than two miles, I would think."

Mason grit his teeth. "That's very close, and there's not much cover nearby."

"I think I may have an answer for that as well. I can electronically camouflage the van to render it invisible to satellite surveillance very easily. If we can get to a location with sufficient cover, we should be able to set up within a mile of the airbase safely."

"Jack me back in," Mason said, donning the I/O. "I'll find something."

* * *

They walked up the overgrown track from the cabin for a while, chatting about nothing in particular. Meeker breathed deeply of the fresh air, savoring the hint of pine it carried. The regular cadence of their stride lulled her pleasantly and Andrew's voice had a soft, calming quality. Everything combined to dull her awareness so that it was several seconds before she realized what he was saying.

"I know some people," he went on. "They can get us new identities, some money. By this time next week we can be in the Rioplex. You'll like it there."

She stopped. "What?"

"It's one of the richest on the south continent," he continued, smiling at her. "There would be plenty..."

"Wait," she said, holding up her hand to stop him going on. "What about Mason and the rest?"

He shrugged, still smiling. "What about them?"

"What about...? And the mission?"

The smile disappeared. "Janice, you know their plan won't work."

"Maybe not, but Populus will think of something."

"Like what?" He stepped closer, spoke quietly, patiently.

"Janice, you don't belong with these people. They don't own you and you don't owe them anything."

She stared at him, confused. "What are you saying?"

His quick smile was back. "This war of theirs doesn't have to include you. Mason, Tripp, the ones calling themselves Knights, they're part of it and can't get loose. They're in too deep."

"And Stephen? What about him?"

Nicholson looked at her sadly. "I did owe him a debt, but haven't I already paid that? I gave up everything – my position, my wealth, my future – to pay back your friends for saving my life." He sighed. "I just want to start over somewhere my past won't find me. Be a different person. Someone not ruled by lust for money and power." He looked into her eyes, held them for a moment. "I want a second chance. And I want you to share it with me."

"Andrew, I..." She tore her eyes away. She couldn't look at him, couldn't bear to see the need in his face.

How did she get here? Why had she been so blind to where she was going? She loved Stephen, but he had never spoken to her this way. She knew he felt deeply for her, but would he walk away from all this just to be with her? Here was a man starting a new life, stretching out his hand to offer her one as well. A chance to begin again, to forget about the intrigue, the fear, the danger, and have an ordinary existence. She wanted to be part of something greater than herself, but what good would it do her, really, if Mason and his cell actually did what they set out to do? Would she become like Jaelon, clutching an ancient memento of a love long lost? At least Jaelon had the comfort of her Vision to sustain her. Janice Meeker had only herself and what little experience her few years offered.

Would it be so wrong to just keep walking down this path with Andrew? Would they even know she was gone?

"Janice?"

"Please, Andrew, I need some time."

He nodded at that. "I guess it is a lot to ask. At least promise me to think about it?"

She managed to give him a weak smile. "I will," she said. To be honest, she knew it would be all she *could* think about for some time.

5

The seed had been planted at least, Nicholson thought. There was already a bit of a rift between the girl and Overguard. The big Texan was plainly jealous of her attention to him. If he was to be successful, he needed to widen that gap until Meeker could see no reason to resist him. It would be her choice to come along. Who knows? Maybe later she might even...

But that was for the future. Now he needed to start the ball rolling if he was to get away from these people before they moved again. There wouldn't be a better time or place to get out. The cabin's isolation might make it difficult to get back to civilization, but he didn't really have a choice.

Overguard was standing by himself against the front wall, scowling at Populus. Something was going on between them, something less than friendly. Could he use that?

Nicholson strolled over to the Greek, who sat at his

computer, oblivious. The screen was a jumble of indecipherable code. Nicholson watched quietly until Populus started and looked around at him.

"Mr. Nicholson! You gave me a turn. May I help you?"

"Oh, no," Nicholson replied with a casual grin. "Just milling about. What's that?" He pointed at the screen.

Populus returned to his work. "I am working on some security protocols."

Nicholson waited for him to elaborate, but the Knight remained silent. He leaned in closer and spoke quietly.

"Security protocols?" he prompted.

Populus nodded.

"Ours, or...?"

The Knight looked sideways at him. "This is very difficult work, Mr. Nicholson. I don't mean to be rude, but..."

"Of course. Sorry." He moved off a few feet. Populus went back to his work without another word. Nicholson made a show of looking around before allowing his gaze to come to rest on Overguard. The man was scowling suspiciously at him. He quickly averted his eyes and stepped smartly toward the kitchen area, noting out of the corner of his eye how Overguard's scowl deepened and his eyes narrowed. Good. The man was becoming convinced he and Populus were connected. Since

Overguard was part of Mason's faction, perhaps a wedge could be driven between him and Jaelon's faction through Overguard. Any disruption within the group could provide him a lever to use against one or the other.

* * *

"Andrew, I've been thinking about what you said."

Nicholson smiled his best at Meeker. He had stepped outside to get some air. The constant closeness of the cabin, crowded with so many people, was beginning to wear on him. His back ached from the sleeping bag and he longed for food that didn't come from boxes and foil. The idea of spending any more time with these people increasingly palled on him.

But he had to hide all that right now. If he could convince Meeker to go with him, the others wouldn't dare follow. Well, none but the Texan, and he was sure Overguard would be easy enough to handle once they were away from the rest.

"Yes?" he asked.

She hesitated. Not a good sign. Alternate plans began spinning in his head.

"I like you, Andrew. I really do."

She's trying to let me down easy, he thought. He hid his amusement behind the smile, not allowing himself to laugh at her pretension. She must a higher estimate of her attractiveness than he had surmised. She was cute, in a primitive way, but nothing like the beauties he'd bedded while the CFO of Catalina Industries.

"It's just, I think I have a duty to the others."

He let the smile drop and feigned disappointment. "It's Overguard, isn't it? You're in love with him."

She nodded slowly, biting her lower lip. He sighed.

"I was afraid of that," he said. "I guess I can understand. But you *do* understand why I have to leave?"

"I think so," she replied with a puzzled frown.

He needed to word this in such a way she wouldn't feel it necessary to run to Mason with the news of his leaving. He needed time to formulate and execute a backup plan.

"I..." He paused to convince her he was just now finding the words although he'd worked out the gist of it already just in case she did refuse. "I can't stay. I don't belong here. Nobody trusts me. No, don't try to deny it. I can see it in their eyes. Janice, I sacrificed everything to help..." He neglected to remind her that Azrael tried to have him killed. "...now I need to start over, but I can't do that here." He took her by the shoulders and held her gaze in his own. "I would have liked you to come with me, to start that new life with you at my side, but I understand. It was too much to ask." He dropped his hands and turned away. "I suppose it's only right; my penance for who I was."

"No, Andrew." She hurried to put a consoling hand on his shoulder. "I can see you are a good man. Don't be so hard on yourself."

He suppressed the smile that threatened to break through. It was time to deliver the final blow. He forced a tragic expression and faced her.

"I can't stay, Janice. I have to go. You understand, don't you?"

"Yes. Yes, of course I do."

"But Mason and the others don't. They'll try to stop me if they find out."

She lifted a hand to her mouth and looked thoughtful.

"You won't tell them, will you Janice?" he pleaded.

She started to say something, then glanced at the cabin door uncertainly.

"Please, Janice," he urged, "I just need another day or so. Maybe just a few hours. I'm not asking you to lie to them, just give me some time."

"Okay," she smiled. "I guess it'll be all right."

He leaned in and gave her a peck on the cheek. "Thanks. I hope someday I can return the kindness."

As she made her way back to the cabin, he gave her a little wave. When he turned away, though, there was a lot more on his mind than Meeker. There was one other person who might be useful.

* * *

Tripp rose and sauntered toward the kitchen to refill his glass. The need to get away was growing. He had promised Mason he would stay until Catalina Industries was taken down, and he had done that. Why was he still here? Did he really want to get involved in this next step? His offer to go in Nicholson's place had been on impulse, a kind of reflex action born of being a part of so many campaigns in the past. He hadn't really thought it out, and when Jaelon had to explain to him why only Nicholson could have accomplished that particular task, it sank in to him that he wasn't really mentally present with the cell any more. All he could think about was the Seraph. It consumed him. It was making him useless, maybe even dangerous to the cell from his inattentiveness.

"Mr. Tripp," Nicholson said from the kitchen door. "It's good to see you up and about."

Nicholson. Just what he needed. "Just going for a refill."

"Please, let me get that for you." Nicholson went into a

cabinet and produced a whiskey bottle. He took Tripp's glass with a smile and poured two fingers of the golden liquid into it. Passing it to Tripp, he went on. "I understand you're leaving us soon." He took another glass from the cabinet and decanted himself a drink.

"Uh huh," Tripp replied, sipping. He wasn't sure how he felt about Nicholson. The Knights seemed to trust him, but they didn't show preference for anyone, so did that really mean anything? He had been critical to the plan against Catalina Industries, and their success had hinged on his actions. He could have turned against them at any point, sabotaged them easily, but he didn't. Maybe the Knights were right after all.

"What do you plan to do afterward, if you don't mind me asking?"

"Well," Tripp said, "I guess I'll go back north. There's still some good land there away from the megaplexes. A lot of it is abandoned farmland. I should be able to find a place to start over."

Nicholson sipped and nodded. "I believe I know something of the area near the New York megaplex. Of course, most of what I know comes from maps and such."

"I'd prefer something closer to the lakes, maybe," Tripp said, warming to the conversation.

They moved back into the front room as they talked.

Tripp noticed Overguard watching them closely. Or was it just Nicholson he was watching?

"You know, I've often thought of something like that myself," Nicholson was saying. "A little place away from it all. A place to think, have time to myself. Put things in perspective, as it were."

"Not just for that," Tripp said. "A place to live. A farm. To feel the earth between your fingers, smell the new-mown hay, raise chickens and cattle..."

Nicholson laughed. "I don't think I could ever do that." He paused and tilted his head at Tripp. "I envy you."

"What? Why?"

"You have the courage they don't," Nicholson said, indicating the others in the cabin.

Tripp scowled, confused. "What do you mean?"

"Striking out on your own. They're hiding from reality, wrapped up in this 'Great Conflict.' You're facing life head-on, unafraid. I envy your courage."

Tripp looked from Nicholson to the others and back. He wondered what exactly the man was getting at. The Conflict was more real than this world created and maintained by deceit and lies.

"I wouldn't say I'm all that brave," he protested. "No more

than anyone else. I just want to live a normal life."

"Oh, I quite understand. Who doesn't?"

"Exactly."

They brought up against the fireplace. Mason glanced at them, then went back to his book. Tripp hovered over his chair, looking from it to Nicholson.

"Please, sit," Nicholson invited. "I can stand."

He looked at Mason and found he didn't want to discuss this in front of the Angelkiller. It didn't seem right.

"Tell you what," he said to Nicholson, "I could use some air. I've been sitting here too long, anyway."

Nicholson shrugged. "Fine with me."

They walked outside, stepping off the front porch to stand in silence, looking at the view.

"I have a confession to make," Nicholson said suddenly.

"Oh?"

"I was going to use those files against Azrael so I could start over."

Tripp kept his expression carefully neutral. They had assumed Nicholson was going to use the stolen information for simple blackmail, but this was more than that. Could they have been wrong? Considering everything they'd seen about Nicholson, it was entirely possible the man had indeed meant to break away from Azrael. Since the Minion would certainly never allow it willingly, maybe stealing the files was the only way.

"I guess I didn't think it through well enough," the man was saying. "I should have known Azrael would have a spy in my office." He laughed bitterly, shaking his head. "My personal secretary."

Tripp took a sip from his drink. This was a strange turn of events. He wondered what Mason would make of it.

"So, here I am," Nicholson went on, "in the middle of nowhere. You know, this is the first time I've been this far from civilization."

"We're not *that* far."

Nicholson chuckled. "Sure looks like it to me."

"There's a little village only about five miles or so west of here," he objected. "Where did you think those power lines came from?"

The other looked at the overhead lines. A small bluebird cocked its head at them from its perch on the wire.

"I really never thought about it," Nicholson admitted. "All the power lines in the megaplexes are underground." He shrugged. "So, five miles, huh? That's not so bad."

Tripp started to agree, but the world suddenly caved in on him.

* * *

A little later, Tripp staggered in from the front yard, holding his head.

"Sorry, Jonah," he said, nursing a large lump on his scalp. "I guess I really screwed up this time." He made his way to the high-backed chair and sank into it.

"I'll get something for that," Meeker volunteered, heading for the kitchen.

"What happened?" Mason asked.

"Never mind that. Where's Nicholson?" Overguard interrupted.

Tripp squinted at them in pain. "I think he hit me and left." He sucked in his breath as Meeker applied a cold compress to his injury. "The last thing I remember is him talking to me about the power lines."

"It's a wonder you can remember anything through the booze," Overguard grunted sourly.

"Stephen!" Meeker snapped.

Overguard shook his head and lapsed into a sullen silence.

"That's it, then," Mason said. "Ready or not, we have to move."

"We are not going after him?" Malthusan put in. "He

cannot have gone far on foot. I can track him and bring him back before nightfall."

"Why?" Mason asked. "He'd only try to leave again. The next time, he might not settle for just knocking someone out to cover his escape."

"There is one way to be sure," Overguard said.

They all looked at him. He met their disapproval with defiance.

"You know I'm right," he insisted.

"Murder is not an option," Jaelon replied firmly.

"It's not murder. It's self-defense. What? You don't think he wouldn't betray us the first chance he got if it suited him?"

"Oh, Stephen," Meeker sighed.

"That is a possibility," Jaelon admitted, "but there will be no murder."

Overguard pointedly turned away from her and looked to Mason. "What about it?" he demanded. "Are you just going to let Nicholson go?"

Mason grimaced. "I have to agree with Jaelon."

Overguard shook his head in disgust. "You're making a mistake!" he began.

Tripp stepped in hastily. "It's no use fighting amongst ourselves. What's done is done."

"Yes," Populus said. "And we need to make the best use of the rest of the day if we are to be gone before dark."

Mason nodded. "Everyone start packing things into the van. Take what supplies will fit."

The Knights and Tripp set about their work, Meeker fussing at him for getting up. Mason walked to Overguard and looked him in the eye.

"Everyone," he said, firmly.

The two stood glaring at each other until Meeker walked over and laid a hand on Overguard's shoulder.

"Give me a hand?" she asked him.

Overguard didn't shift. "This isn't over, Mason," he growled.

"We can settle it after we've got the others somewhere safe."

"Stephen, please," Meeker insisted, taking his arm and pulling at him.

"Count on it," Overguard shot at Mason as he followed Meeker.

* * *

It was late afternoon before they left the cabin behind. Storm clouds gathered on the western horizon as they made their way back eastward across the broken remains of an old two lane road. Several times Malthusan and Mason had to hack a clear path through thick underbrush that had grown across the way in the decades since the track was last used. Mason was encouraged by the signs of disuse but concerned at their lack of progress. At a narrow point, they found a makeshift bridge spanning the White River, undoubtedly erected by some locals using whatever they could find. Everyone but Populus dismounted and walked across, checking the structure before Mason waved the all clear. In spite of its groans and creaks, they were relieved the bridge bore the weight of the van.

Night fell and the storm broke over them, rendering parts of their way muddy and nearly impassable. The Knights' van rambled gamely along, though, and it became clear they could never have navigated the route without it.

They were finally forced to stop as they reached the Mississippi. The river churned before them, tossed heavily by the storm, lit occasionally by lightning crackling around them. Thunder shook the van. The river was much too wide for any amateurish bridge here, and no ferries had survived the years. The only way across appeared to be the old interstate bridge, but that led directly into the Memphisplex.

"It seems this is where we stop for the time being,"

Populus said from his seat at the controls. "Crossing the river now would be too dangerous."

"I hope Andrew is all right," Meeker said. She glanced at Overguard, who looked away with a frown.

"He is not our problem any longer," Malthusan said, peering into the storm's murk.

Lightning sparked, immediately followed by a deafening thunderclap. They all jumped.

"That was close," Tripp observed when the ringing in their ears had subsided.

Jaelon made her way to the back of the van. "Best settle in," she said. She produced a couple of inflatable mattresses from storage compartments. "I suggest two on, four off."

"Agreed," said Malthusan, turning away from the darkened rain. "I will take first and third watch."

* * *

"I think it is safe to cross," Populus said.

The storm hadn't ended, but its rage had abated, leaving a swollen river stretching between them and the Memphisplex. Populus and Tripp stood looking out at the Mississippi, blinking rainwater from their eyes in the waning downpour. The sound of the rain on their waterproof camo clothing was a soothing light drumming.

"Now?" Tripp asked.

The Greek nodded. "It would not be wise to wait until the rain has completely stopped. The megaplex's surveillance drones will be back up soon."

"Okay, but how? You don't have a boat, and that's a long swim."

Populus grinned at him. "Come with me."

They went to the van and Populus motioned him to take hold of a protuberance barely visible in the vehicle's skin.

"Twist left and pull," he instructed.

There was a whine from within the body of the van as he complied. He stepped back as a section of the van's side panel running from the driver's door to the rear separated and swung outward. Populus manipulated a control near the front door and was rewarded with a loud hissing noise. A portion of the exposed panel expanded into a pontoon shape.

"Very nice," he said.

"Now the other side," the Knight said. "It is not really much of an innovation," he continued as they inflated the other pontoon. "Amphibious vehicles have been around for centuries."

"Is there anything this van can't do?" he asked.

"Very little," Populus said. "After all, it pays to be prepared when facing an enemy like Azrael."

"It'll be light soon," Tripp observed as they locked the pontoons in place. "Can you get across in time?"

"I believe so," the Knight answered, then paused as he realized what Tripp just said. "Are you not coming with us?"

Tripp sighed. They would have to know. Once they were across the river, he wouldn't get another chance. He couldn't get involved in another campaign, and he knew if he went with them this time it would be forever. His heart wasn't in it any more. All he could think about was getting away, finding a normal life in some out of the way place to spend his last days. It wasn't as if they really needed him any more. They had the Knights. And after the way he'd screwed up with Nicholson... No, it was best he left now. That way, they could concentrate on the task at hand without worrying whether he might throw a wrench in the works.

"I think it's time," he said.

Populus grunted his understanding. "Where will you go?"

"I'm not sure," he admitted. "I told Nicholson I might go north, so that's probably not a good idea now. Maybe I'll head west. Lots of open land that way. Plenty of space to lose yourself, get away from prying eyes and ears."

"I wish you the best," the Knight said, extending his hand to shake. "There are traveling supplies in the van. Take what you need."

"Thanks," Tripp said, taking the proffered hand.

He headed into the van and nearly collided with Meeker coming out. He excused himself and pushed by her. It was beginning to dawn on him that his departure would have more effect than he'd anticipated. As he shuffled through the food lockers, he couldn't help but notice Meeker standing in the van's doorway. He glanced at her once, then went back to his search. He found a duffel bag folded into one of the compartments and opened it. It was at least ten days on foot to the nearest settlement. Best to take two weeks of rations just in case.

"Are you leaving now?"

Meeker had come up quietly beside him and was watching him load the rations into the bag.

"Shortly, yes," he replied without looking at her or pausing in his work.

"Oh."

He finished packing the food and started looking for what camping supplies might be available. She watched in silence for a bit.

"It's been nice working with you," she stumbled. Obviously, she felt she should say something but had no idea how to go about it.

He gave her a smile. "Same here." He packed some ignition supplies and hummed as he scanned the shelves. For a moment he wondered how they managed to always be so well stocked, then shrugged and pulled down a water purification and first aid kit. Populus did say to take whatever he needed.

"Will we see you again?" she asked.

"Probably not," he replied, closing the duffel bag.

Suddenly, she leapt forward and wrapped herself around him. Startled, he dropped the bag and caught her in his arms.

"Be safe, be safe," she murmured, her face buried in his shoulder.

Then she disentangled and ran from the van, leaving him stunned and befuddled. After a moment, he shook himself and picked up the bag. He would never understand women. All the time Meeker had been with their group, she hadn't said more than a few words to him, but apparently she was at least a little fond of him, else what was that about?

He stepped out of the van and found Jaelon waiting for him.

"You are sure this is what you want to do?" she asked

without preamble.

He looked around. Meeker was crying into Overguard's chest. The Texan looked at him and nodded solemnly. That was probably as much as he would get in the way of goodbye from the man. Tripp nodded back.

"Yes," he told Jaelon. "I think it's best I leave before you cross the river. I would only be in the way over there."

She stepped up to him and embraced him shortly, then stepped back.

"Farewell, Jonathan Prester," she said.

He was a little surprised to hear his birth name after so many years. But, why should he be? The Knights knew many things hidden from most. It was both disconcerting and comforting. They were agents of the Master, after all, privy to a lot more than he would ever be this side of the veil. He smiled at her as Malthusan appeared beside her.

"Take care and be well," the Cypriot Knight wished him.

"Thanks." He glanced around again. There was one more goodbye to say, the hardest of them all.

* * *

Mason had walked around to the other side of the van to smoke. The rain had reduced to a light shower, more a warm caress than a drenching. He heard someone come around the van toward him and knew without looking who it had to be. He puffed on the cigar without acknowledging Tripp's presence. There could be only one reason Tripp was there. The time had come at last.

They had been friends, comrades-in-arms, for a long time. He'd come to take it for granted Tripp would always be at his side. How had he let that happen? Years ago he'd promised himself not to get attached to anyone. The ephemeral nature of human life had too often led to heartache. Was it because Tripp's case was so different, because they shared a place in the Conflict? Was that what had convinced him to ignore that one rule?

"It's for everyone's safety, Jonah," Tripp said.

He knew Tripp was right, but did that mean he had to agree? They had lost Chandler and Martin. After being together for nearly three centuries, Tripp had become as familiar as any family might be to him. Now it felt like the cell was falling apart, a family breaking up.

"Well, say *something*," Tripp urged, "anything!"

He took the cigar and examined the ash on its end. They were all just ashes, weren't they? Their lives ended in ashes. Their relationships ended in ashes. Time and circumstance were merciless, uncaring.

"Remember Nevada?" he asked.

Tripp frowned, then nodded. "That was a long time ago, Jonah. That Minion was nothing like Azrael and we didn't have Knights to help."

"I know."

"So what is it, then?"

What, indeed? "You saved my life, John."

Tripp shook his head at that. "And how many times have you done the same for me?"

"It's not a matter of keeping score," Mason said, trying hard to find the right words. "We've worked together against some very high odds. I'm just finding it hard to believe you would walk away now."

Tripp's response was sharp. "Hey, don't forget, Jonah, I volunteered for this." Mason could hear the hurt in the other's voice and regretted his own choice of words. "I walked in of my own free will," Tripp went on. "Is it so hard to believe I would walk out the same way?"

"I don't want you to think I'm stopping you. I'm just trying to understand why you want to leave." He took a breath and grappled with his thoughts. They should have had this conversation long before. It shouldn't have been left until now. He didn't have time to formulate all the questions to get all the answers he wanted. Tripp was about to do what he himself had wanted to do for years. He must have found those answers. "Is it that you haven't found what you were looking for? Is it that what we're doing isn't worth it to you anymore?"

"No, it's not that at all. Working with you and the others has done more to make my life full than I ever could have alone. Signing on with you opened my eyes to the Truth. If it weren't for you, I would never have seen any place outside New England." He waved a hand toward the van and the people on the other side. "I'd never have met people like this. I'd never have seen the Seraph."

There it was. The fixed point, what had happened that had brought this all about. "That's just it. You weren't supposed to see it, John. You weren't even supposed to be there."

"Are you sure? Don't things happen for a reason?" Tripp placed a hand on his shoulder. "Look, old friend, I would like to retire, but if you need me I'll stay. All you have to do is ask. There will be no hard feelings. I'll do my best to help, you know that."

Mason hung his head. "I know. I do know that." He couldn't look up. Tripp might be staring at him, and that would stop him saying what he knew was right. His friend had earned this, there was no denying. Who was he to say no?

"I will miss you," he managed to say.

Tripp squeezed his shoulder. "Me, too. Who knows? Some time in the near future, if all goes well, you'll stop by a little farm in the Midwest and visit. My door will always be open." He hesitated another moment, then gave Mason a pat on the shoulder. "Goodbye, my friend. Be well and take care of yourself."

"Yeah, you too," was all Mason trusted himself to say. He shoved the cigar back between his teeth to stop saying any more. He didn't lift his head until he heard Tripp walk away. He fought down the lump in his throat and tasted bitterness. He looked at the cigar.

It had gone out.

* * *

Populus came around the van a few minutes later. He stood patiently until Mason sighed and walked over to him.

"We're ready," the Greek told him.

"Tripp gone?"

"Yes. He just left, headed west."

Mason nodded sadly.

"I'm sorry," Populus said gently.

He shook himself and turned his attention to the future.

There was much to be done, and time enough for looking back later.

"Right, then, let's go."

Populus turned and they walked back around to join the others. "The current will no doubt take us downstream quite a ways, but we should still be able to beach well north of the megaplex perimeter."

"How close to the base will that put us?" Mason asked.

Populus scowled. "It is hard to say exactly. Five miles. Six, perhaps."

Mason grunted unhappily. "What about cover?"

"The area is still heavily forested. We should be able to find an old road or trail to follow while remaining hidden from satellite and drone detection."

"Very well," Mason said. "Let's load up."

The campsite was clean, Mason noticed. He was the last into the van.

Populus cranked the engine. "Buckle in, everyone. This is going to be exciting."

6

Azrael sat glumly reviewing what little information he had on Mason's cell.

With the loss of Catalina Industries, his intelligence network in North America had been heavily crippled. Only now did he realize how extensively Nicholson's web had been spun, a web that collapsed with his death. The power vacuum left by his demise had yet to be filled, a situation that must soon be rectified, but not before even more pressing matters were handled. The best he could do for now was keep the North American cells, including Mason's, off guard and busy.

He jacked into his I/O set. Immediately he found himself in the comm center of Andlat Enterprises, the most heavily secured branch of his empire. Only he and two others had access to this VR, the Minion interrogating Martin and the one in charge of his field operations.

The room looked crowded with people working busily at consoles announcing themselves as channels to key locations around the globe, but none of the avatars were controlled by actual people. The center was completely automated, creating humanoid avatars as a convenience for interface. Each avatar was programmed to appear as a native of the region to which its channel connected.

He hailed the avatar for the North American bloc, the one dressed in the khaki of a late twentieth century United States naval officer. The avatar snapped to attention and saluted.

"Report on known Army cells," he barked at it.

"Twenty-five are located and under surveillance, sir."

"How many in the central portion?"

"Ten, sir."

"Dispatch five teams. Kill them all. Destroy any contacts. I want maximum disruption to start within 48 hours."

"Yes, sir."

The avatar turned toward its console. Indicators began lighting up across its board. Azrael nodded to himself. The death squads would spread terror across the central megaplexes. That should keep even Mason's cell busy long enough to put things in motion. If might even flush them out of hiding. However it went, once the plan reached a certain point, even the loss of

Andlat Enterprises wouldn't stop the inevitable. The Conflict would finally come to an end, and his master would be the undisputed owner of this world.

Azrael wondered just how the master would reward him for this. Perhaps he would allow him to kill Mason and his troublesome group personally.

* * *

They arrived at the new location shortly before dark and set up the satlink. Jaelon and Malthusan went out to recon and establish a secure perimeter while Mason and his group set up the camo tents by the van. In less than an hour they were ready to start the next phase of the plan: connecting into the military base's network.

"You're sure this will work?" Overguard said, eying Populus closely.

"Absolutely," the Knight assured him. "I have already surveyed their security protocols. Child's play."

Overguard grunted skeptically.

"Come away, Stephen," Meeker said, taking his arm. "Let the man work."

The Texan reluctantly allowed himself to be led away toward the mess tent. Mason passed them as he made his final round of checks. Overguard ignored the man's nod. He still couldn't fathom why Mason let Nicholson go free. It made no sense to allow the man to leave knowing what he did about them.

"Stephen?"

He looked at her. She was holding out a glass to him. It smelled of caffeine and creme. He took it and thanked her.

"Are you still sore about Andrew?" she asked.

He sipped the drink and looked away. Yes, he was, and not just because he left them. But how could he admit that to her? How would she take the fact he had been jealous the whole time Nicholson was with them? It seemed so petty now, that he had ever doubted her. He felt more than a little ashamed he hadn't trusted her.

"It's okay," she said, taking his face in her hands. "I understand."

"Do you?" he replied, a bit more sharply than he meant.

She kissed him lightly on the lips. "Yes. I do."

He wanted to step away from her, give himself time to sort out all that had happened in the last few hours. He wanted to find a quiet spot away from them all, but she wouldn't let him pull away. She wrapped her arms around his neck.

"I love you," she said, searching his face.

He put the glass down and disentangled himself from her embrace.

"I just need some time," he began. "I..."

Words failed him. He was confused. Confused about his feelings for her, for their work, for everything. What did he really expect from it all? What had they become, working for Azrael, taking in Nicholson? What had he become?

She stood quietly watching him. Did she expect him to say something? What? That he loved her, too? Did he really have to say it? Didn't he show it to her every day? Didn't he put her ahead of himself in everything? Try to protect her always? Didn't she know he would take a bullet for her without thinking twice? How could she not?

"I need time," he repeated. "It's not that I don't trust you, Janice. It's just..." He looked away. How could he explain it so she would understand? "I'm having a hard time trusting these other people now." He was ashamed to admit even to himself the depth of his jealousy. Who was he to deny her her own choice?

"Stephen, I need you to know something." She took a deep breath. "Andrew asked me to go with him. I refused."

Her admission stunned him on several levels. The thought of Nicholson leaving never bothered him, but that he'd tried to get her to go along made him boil.

"When was this?" he asked, a bit more roughly than he intended.

"Does it matter? I turned him down. Isn't that what matters?"

He nearly bit his tongue trying not to blurt out a retort. Instead, he reached for her and pulled her close.

"Yes," he said, his voice hoarse in his own ears. "That's what matters."

She snuggled deeper into his arms. "Mad at me?"

"What? No, of course not."

"Good."

He held her for a little, letting the moment seep into his soul. Her quiet stilled the unease that had been building inside him. The peace he felt was something he hadn't known for some time, probably wouldn't as long as he stayed with Mason and his people. Maybe the idea of leaving wasn't so bad after all.

"Janice?"

"Yes?"

"Would you leave with me if I asked?"

She turned her face up to his. "Is that what you want?"

He started to say something, then found he wasn't sure. He looked around. The others were busy with their own problems.

He and Janice were almost outsiders anyway. Mason treated her like a child and him like a servant.

"Stephen?"

"Not right now, but soon," he told her. He had to be sure Mason didn't... what? Betray them to Azrael? Get someone else killed because of a bad decision?

"Whenever you want," she promised.

"You won't mind leaving the others?"

She shook her head. "When Andrew asked me, I did a lot of thinking about that. They don't really enter into it, do they? I mean, they survived before I came along. I'm sure they could adapt to our leaving."

He frowned at her. "If you think that way, why did you turn Nicholson down?"

She tilted her head at him and smiled. "Because I don't love him."

He couldn't help but kiss her then. He told her in that kiss what he couldn't say put into words just yet. His gratitude for her support. His need for her affection. His desire for her nearness and a longing for her respect. She responded with a warm kiss of her own. The embrace became something more than just the proximity of their bodies. It became a joining of their souls. The depth of that feeling drew the phrase from him he'd wanted to share but had been afraid to venture for fear she would deny him.

"I love you, too," he found he could admit aloud. "I want you for my wife." Once said, he wondered why it had been so difficult.

He felt her tense for a second at the statement. Was it shock? Was she about to pull away, tell him he had misunderstood? A thrill of dread went through him.

"Yes, my love," she said, holding him tighter. "Oh, yes."

He just held her for a long moment, the scent of her touching him to his core. He allowed himself to believe this was forever, this single perfect second. It might be a dream, but dreams were what made life worthwhile. If he could have just this one moment to remember, then he could carry it with him the rest of his life and be content.

7

It wasn't much, but it was enough to notice. Had he been facing any other way, he probably would have missed it.

Each time, just before the beast charged, the woman made a furtive movement with her left or right hand. Knight Maachen kicked himself. Of course, this was only virtual reality after all. She was controlling the beast. She was its operator. It could never be beaten because it was nothing but an image, a construct. But she, on the other hand, was a different story. No doubt she was using the same kind of advanced interface he was. That meant...

He forced himself to turn away from the beast and launched at her.

Startled, she hesitated only a second then blinked out, leaving Maachen to stab at empty air. He spun, hoping against hope he had guessed right.

He was alone. The beast had disappeared.

* * *

The reconnaissance project proceeded as planned. Within a week, they had a system built that could monitor any active terminal on the grid. They slowly developed a database of critical financial and social information on Andlat Enterprises.

It soon became apparent Andlat Enterprises was not just a large corporation. Connections with highly placed government officials all over the world showed up regularly. Covert operations, including arms sales, drugs, and human trafficking information passed through the network in angelic script, which Mason lost no time in translating.

Azrael was definitely a very accomplished and powerful criminal. No surprise there. What did surprise them was the extent of Azrael's involvement in the growing unrest in Europe and the Middle East.

They discovered Andlat Enterprises had several ghost companies, or "beards," in the Persian Empire, where they moved millions of euros from Western corporations into Persian companies that would otherwise have failed. Azrael was nearly single-handedly keeping two nations' economies afloat while bankrolling another five terrorist organizations. Should he be effectively eliminated, the Persian Empire might not be mortally wounded, but it would be heavily crippled.

Suddenly, their mission was no longer just a personal exoneration for Mason. Its scope had broadened to include more than just his own reconciliation, and he was ashamed of his self-centeredness. He determined to not just remove Azrael from his seat atop Andlat Enterprises but bring down the whole thing. All he had to do was convince the others.

"You're crazy. You know that," Overguard said.

"May be," Mason admitted. "But if my madness saves lives, does it make a difference?"

Meeker laughed. Overguard shot her an annoyed look.

"With all we have, it should be fairly simple to just sabotage Andlat operations," Populus said. "We can come at it from dozens of ways simultaneously. Azrael can't plug all the holes at once."

"Taking out Andlat is just the first step," Mason said. "We're going to push The Enemy out of VR and more."

"Pretty ambitious," Overguard scoffed. "How are you going to succeed where everyone has failed?"

Mason glared at him. "This Conflict has gone on for too long. It has stolen lives, taken from humanity what little had remained after the Fall. The Enemy wreaks misery on us and feeds on our despair. For centuries, we've told ourselves we could never hope to stand against The Enemy because they have the authority they usurped when they rebelled. I let myself believe the same thing for a long time. I watched as the world fell farther and farther under the influence of the Dark, excusing my cowardice by saying what can one man do? It wasn't until I met Tripp..." He stopped. He was going off on a tangent, one he hadn't meant to share. He took a breath and started again. "Well, it is past time their judgment caught up with them. Now, I may not be able to pull this off, Stephen, but for more than two thousand years I've watched people I knew, and some I loved, come and go in a world that held no joy for them." He fought the lump rising in his throat, surprised at his own words. Where had this come from?

Meeker and Overguard sat looking at him with stunned expressions. He couldn't blame them. In all the time they'd known him, he'd never opened up. He was their leader, the Angelkiller. He wasn't supposed to be like them. He was old. He was eternal. He wasn't really human in their eyes. To them, it must have been difficult to tell him apart from The Enemy.

Again he felt keenly that alienation, from them and from his own humanity. At last he saw that what he'd thought was the weight of his age was actually the burden of loneliness, a loneliness that began when his mentor died and had compounded every moment since. The deaths of his family, his comrades, the losses throughout the years had made him give up hope of finding a companion to share his life, a life that of necessity became more about the Conflict, more about The Enemy than about himself. He had become, in their eyes and somehow in his own, a symbol of the Conflict itself. Immortal. Unending. Invulnerable. Undying.

A great sorrow hit him and grief clouded his eyes. He had been so busy surviving, so caught up in looking after the welfare of those he considered his charges, he had stopped considering himself. He looked at his compatriots through new eyes, reborn eyes, cleared by the release of guilt that until then lay like a pall over his consciousness. He found Jaelon's hand on his shoulder and saw understanding in her eyes. Had it been anyone else, he wouldn't have believed there was any truth behind that, but the Knight knew the loneliness as well as he. If there was anything Mason shared with the Knights, it was that.

"I understand," he continued. "Believe me, I understand how you feel, but there are things happening today, forces in motion that are bigger than anything we have seen before." He paused to consider his next words because they would voice a question that had been haunting him for some time. "Why do you think, Stephen, that there are not one but three Knights here with us?"

Overguard's expression told him exactly what the man was thinking. The man had indeed considered the import of that circumstance. Mason wondered precisely what Overguard had surmised. He caught Jaelon's gaze, noting the carefully neutral expression there. Undaunted, he went on.

"The Conflict is escalating, this we know for sure," he told them, still looking at Jaelon's impassive visage. Her lack of reaction irritated him unaccountably. "I do not intend to sit on the sidelines if we can use what we know to help bring the Conflict closer to an end." Jaelon lifted an eyebrow at him. Mason could almost hear her skepticism, but went on. "We will hit Andlat Enterprises and all its subsidiaries simultaneously, inside the system and out."

Populus spoke up at that. "Inside the system we can do, no problem. But outside?"

"We need to coordinate with the European and Asian cells, show them what we have," Mason said.

"I don't know," Overguard interrupted. "Rome is iffy at best. And London was not very excited last time I talked to them."

Jaelon stepped forward. "Then, we will take the case to them personally." She looked at Mason. "I will go to England.

Malthusan can take Rome." To Overguard, she asked, "Will that suffice?"

Overguard stiffly bowed his head to her, then awkwardly cleared his throat and turned away.

* * *

Azrael's death squads began operating in five North American cities within thirty-six hours of his command. Within seventy-two hours they had spread terror across the continent, inflicting hundreds of casualties in the Chicago, Saint Louis, Memphis, Little Rock, and New Orleans megaplexes.

Azrael read the results with satisfaction. Surely the Army cells would take action to at least try to alleviate the threat. It was simply a matter of time. Once they showed themselves, they would be eradicated.

He was less pleased with the progress against Martin. He found it hard to believe the cripple was still holding out against his interrogator. With more important matters pressing, he was reluctant to take over the questioning himself. There was the supervision of the Persian advance's supply to consider, a task he didn't want to trust to anyone else, so he had assigned what should have been a simple task to one of his underlings.

While he worked behind the scenes to stir up the conflict,

publicly he needed to maintain his distance from the Persian belligerence issue for appearance sake. So it was he spent most of his time keeping a high profile in the New York office, tending to Andlat Enterprises' philanthropic efforts or the business of supplying raw materials for the continental megaplexes' food processors. With farming and food distribution done nearly exclusively from the African plains since the turn of the century, Andlat Enterprises had become the major handler of global comestibles. China's farms were his biggest competitors, but the sheer logistics of moving billions of tons of perishables a month had kept their successes against Andlat's interests to a minimum. With the outbreak of hostilities in the West and its inevitable impact on the movement of good globally, Andlat had all but gained a monopoly on that market, just as he planned.

Azrael had worked for decades to maneuver Andlat into this position, and just when it was all about to pay off, Jenkins and his Catalina Industries cronies had thrown a wrench in the works. Using Mason's Army cell against Jenkins had given him the time he needed to start the ball rolling toward war in the European Bloc, but if he was to expand the conflict further into the West with any chance of success he needed to neutralize the very people he had recruited. Their ability to completely shut down Catalina Industries' network told him that the information they got from Jenkins before Catalina went under could be a real threat to Andlat at large. That threat had to be eliminated and soon. The best chance he had of doing that rotated around breaking Martin.

He logged on to his network and again found himself in the comm center. The level of activity was much heightened from his previous visit. A good sign that all was proceeding well. He approached a female avatar wearing dark clothing. A coiled dragon emblem adorned her blouse above the left breast. She turned to face him, her face blank.

"Report," he barked.

"Working," she replied impassively.

He waited for her to expound on that, but she said nothing more.

"Progress!" he pressed.

"None," she admitted, still impassive.

The avatar's operator wasn't even logged in, he realized. It was hard to tell if that was good or bad news. Azrael growled in irritation. Must he go there personally to insure this got done?

He walked to the console beside the avatar and scanned its readout. It was a mass of incomprehensible symbols, no use at all to him. Could it be the operator was hiding something from him? He wondered. He turned back to the avatar.

"Directive."

"Ready," came the flat reply.

"Report immediately or be replaced."

"Directive understood."

The avatar froze in place. He knew the operator's station was alarming. To ignore that would invite dire consequences. As the seconds ticked by without a response he began a slow burn.

Abruptly, the avatar shivered. It straightened and a marked transformation took place. The operator's input gave it a more life-like appearance. Its motions became fluid and its flat expression took on the semblance of a harried and anxious underling.

"Yes sir?"

"Report your progress," he repeated, fuming.

"We are very close to breaking him."

"What's taking so long?"

The avatar hesitated. "He is much stronger than we expected."

"Not good enough!" he said. This had gone on too long. The rest of his plan would have to wait because of the incompetence of this woman. Fury burned in him.

"Sir, I..."

"Prepare to receive me tomorrow," he interrupted. "I will take over the interrogation myself."

The avatar bowed. "Yes sir."

He logged off, ignoring the abrupt transition and momentary disorientation. He threw the I/O set across the office. It shattered against the far wall. He cursed violently and the temperature in the room plummeted, frosting the windows' interiors. The scent of lilac flooded the office.

The door opened and three men spilled into the room, weapons drawn. He glowered at them.

"Get out!" he roared.

The guards scrambled over each other in their haste to escape.

* * *

Nicholson was exhausted.

After all his planning, it had come down to just taking advantage of an opportunity dropped in his lap. When Tripp told him about the little settlement so close by, he knew he had found the answer to his dilemma. Once he got back to civilization, he would get in touch with his contacts and start the process of recovery. It was more than he hoped for.

He'd rendered Tripp unconscious with a single blow

and set out immediately, without a thought for any other preparation. After all, it was only five miles. It wouldn't take that long.

Drenched, muddy, and starving, he finally stumbled into the little store advertising "Last Chance for Real Food."

"My God, man!" the storekeeper, a man in his late sixties with little hair and an ample middle said, rushing to meet him at the door. "What happened? Are ya all right?"

"My flier crashed about five miles out," he lied. "Do you have a commset?"

The man helped him to a seat near a counter top crowded with with canned goods.

"Sorry, son. Near'st one's in Little Rock."

Nicholson sighed. It figured. He knew it wasn't going to be easy to get back to civilization, but he didn't count on it being this hard. How did these people survive being so isolated?

"Is there any way to get there besides walking?" he asked.

The man chuckled. "Thur's a transit leavin' tomorra fer the Jacksonville sector. But ya don't look like yer in enny shape..."

He waved off the storekeeper's concern. "I'll be fine. Give me a chance to clean up and I'll be on my way."

"Nonsense! There ain't nowhere 'round ta stay but here,

lessen ya wanna walk ta Mountain Home, an' that's another ten mile." He stepped into the doorway that led to a back room. "Martha! Martha, put another plate on fer dinner. We got comp'ny."

"No, really. I wouldn't want to put you out."

"Pshaw, young'un. Ain't no trouble. Happy ta have ya."

An elderly woman came in and peered at him through her cataracts, clutching a dish towel in gnarled hands. "What's this?"

"Boy's flitter crashed a little ways up," the storekeeper explained. He returned to Nicholson. "This here's ma wife, Martha. I'm Bert."

"Andrew."

"Well, Andrew, reckon ya'll be stayin' the night."

Nicholson nodded and took his first good look around. The little store wasn't much more than a single room lined with metal shelving. Canned goods crowded most of the space. There were a few wooden crates filled with things that looked something like the pictures of vegetables he'd seen, but these had spots and were not quite the pristine colors he was familiar with. Was that what they were offering to feed him?

"You okay, son?" Bert asked, concerned. "Ya look a bit green."

Nicholson swallowed hard. "I'm fine. Still a little shook up I guess."

"A hot bath and a good meal'll fix that," Martha told him. "Come on through."

He wasn't sure about the meal, but the hot bath did sound good. He followed her into the back room.

The room was darker than the front and it took a few seconds for his eyes to adjust. He heard Martha close the door and the click of the lock. He was about to turn to ask her what was going on when the other figure in the room came into focus.

He recognized her instantly. How could he not? She had been his secretary for years, his confidant, almost a lover. She had also been the one Mason's cell said tried to kill him there in that bar, leaving him critically wounded.

"Jessie?"

"Hello, Andrew."

"What are you doing here?"

She ignored the question. "That will be all, Martha."

The old woman unlocked the door, went through and locked it behind her.

"Now, Andrew," Jessie said, "let's talk." She smiled at him. "You're a hard man to find, but I figured you would eventually tire of their company. All I had to do was wait."

She produced a weapon from within her coat and pointed it at him. "When our team followed up at the bar and we found out they'd taken you, we guessed you might not be dead. Then when Catalina Industries failed we knew for certain. Only one person had enough knowledge of its operations to do that. We spread agents all over this area. It was most accomodating of you to stumble into my little store."

"Look," Nicholson said. He thought quickly. What would she believe? She was loyal to Azrael, that he knew. "I don't know what you're thinking, but you have to understand they forced me to work with them. I didn't want to. Hell, I only went to the meeting in the bar to recover the information they stole from Jenkins."

"Is that so?"

"Sure. I wanted to show Azreal that Jenkins was acting on his own. Look, I had no idea he had stolen the information until I was contacted by Mason and his people."

She tilted her head at him. "And once you had the information, you were going to turn it over to Azreal?"

He laughed nervously. Was she buying it? "Of course. I'm no fool."

She chuckled at that. "Neither am I."

"Hey, I can still be useful," he said, backing up against the door. He gasped as she leveled the weapon at his head. "I'll tell you everything I know about them. You're making a mistake!"

"Sorry, Andrew. I have my orders."

The shot reverberated through the little back room.

8

She was back. He brought his shield up between them.

"So, the time for games is over," she said. "I had hoped I wouldn't have to resort to these measures, but you have left me little choice. Time is running out, Martin. Our patience is gone. This is your last chance."

Was that a hint of fear and desperation he heard in her voice? What was going on outside? A wild hope rose in him.

"What's wrong?" he goaded. "Things getting hot?"

She scowled. Without a word, she waved a hand at him. He felt a blow that knocked him backward and left him dazed. She waved again and things got blurry as he lifted a few feet then slammed hard into the ground.

* * *

The crimson streaks breaking the black of the night sky over

Vienna were not the signs of a coming dawn. They were the opening shots of invasion.

Shells fell on Vienna for nearly three hours before the first Imperial fliers streaked overhead to deliver their payloads of death. The defenders barely had time to raise a token resistance before they were reduced to ash by tactical nuclear strikes. It soon became clear the Imperials were less interested in gaining territory than in a swift and decisive victory.

Swarming ahead of the enemy advance, a panicked flood of refugees choked the countryside between the falling megaplexes. People who had never ventured more than a few miles from home for generations scattered blindly to starve or die of exposure as the combat doggedly pursued them across the landscape. In a matter of days, the formerly scenic environment of the European Bloc's eastern stretches became a blasted, smoking ruin littered with unburied dead. Entire cities collapsed before the onslaught, reduced to less than rubble. The achievements of centuries utterly obliterated in seconds by an implacable, uncompromising foe.

Frantic pleas for negotiation went unheeded. Hasty alliances were cobbled together between former Western enemies even as Imperial forces marched inexorably across the continent. Imperial fifth columnists, sleeper cells, and saboteurs wrought global terror, revealing just how deeply imbedded they had become and how long the campaign had been planned. Western leaders fell to assassination with appalling frequency, sometimes at the hands of previously trusted associates.

Through it all, the surviving Army cells worked to dismantle The Enemy's infrastructure, trying to attack the root while the outside world struggled against the branches.

* * *

It was inconvenient he couldn't fly directly into the airbase, but to do so would have alerted the local authorities of his activities there. There were too many other Minions embedded in the Memphisplex power structure to chance that one of them might interfere with his plans.

Azrael flew into the Memphis Aerodrome in the corporate flier accompanied by his three bodyguards. The Aerodrome Authority passed him through the security checkpoint with no more than a cursory glance. Persons of his stature were immune to the stringent scrutiny afforded the average citizen. An armored limousine awaited him, flanked by two men in dark suits. One held the door for him as he climbed in. Every move was made in rehearsed efficiency. The bodyguards piled into the trailing car and they left within ten minutes of him, headed to the old airbase where Martin was being held.

Inside the limo, Azrael tapped a panel built into the back of the driver's compartment. The panel slid aside to reveal a workstation comparable to that in the VR comm center. A few quiet commands connected him to the airbase. A holographic image of his operative appeared hovering before him.

"Is everything prepared?" he asked.

"Yes, sir."

"Any change?"

"No, sir."

Azrael grimaced. "Increase the feedback."

"It shall be done."

He motioned a command to sever the connection. The panel slid back into place as he settled back to watch the road go by.

Something was not right. He couldn't put his finger on exactly what that was. Martin's resistance was a surprise. No one had ever gone so long without breaking. Either his operative was losing her touch, in which case she would have to be replaced, or the man had a reserve of strength Azrael had never before encountered. He frowned.

There were rumors he'd always discounted as excuses given by incompetents about agents of the Conflict's other side, people even more formidable than the Angelkillers. He had never yet dealt with one of them. Could this Martin be one? If so, why had he not sensed it when he met with Mason's cell? He vividly remembered the effectiveness of Mason's wards when they first met. The memory of the pain of his misstep that set them off sent a twinge up his spine.

Would such a storied fighter as one of these so-called Knights have allowed himself be captured? And if so, why?

He wished the limo would move faster.

* * *

"What's in the bag?" Mason asked.

Populus closed the locking clasp. Inside were smoke charges, a taser weapon and his signal amplifier. He turned to the rest to tell them the news.

"I think I may have located Martin," he announced.

They stood in amazed silence. He wasn't surprised. Even he had given the man up for lost, yet there it was, the transponder signal from Martin's subcutaneous communicator was loud and clear. Its limited range had fooled them into believing Martin was gone. Once they were close enough, it had begun transmitting and within a few moments he knew the man was alive, at least.

"Where?" Mason asked once he could find his voice.

"Believe it or not, there in the airbase."

Jaelon nodded. "Of course. It would be the closest place to take him for interrogation."

"Indeed," Populus agreed. "For the same reasons we sought out this location, Azrael uses it as a base for his own purpose. It is isolated from the main complexes, yet close enough to tap into the international networks."

"Can we get to him?" Meeker asked.

"There is a chance one of us could get in and out without being detected," Populus said. "A small chance. And since I am the one who knows how to use the signal tracker best, it should be me."

"I don't like it," Overguard groused. "What if Martin is too heavily guarded? What if you get caught?"

"Why, then we are no worse off. The monitors I have installed are set on automatic. If I am captured, all you have to do is hit the upload on the virus when the alarm goes off."

"If it ever goes off," the dour Texan said.

"It will, my friend. It will. It is only a matter of time until my snooper program finds a way into their network."

Jaelon put a hand on Populus' shoulder. "Krato, if you are caught..."

He managed a slight smile. They both knew he wouldn't allow himself to be interrogated by The Enemy. He would die before he that happened, but not without a fight they would long remember.

It was odd, he thought. He had always known that this might happen someday, it just never hit him that today might be that day. He had always worked with Jaelon and Malthusan, never alone, yet this situation demanded it. Both of the other Knights knew the risk he was running. Both knew they could not convince him to avoid it. He wondered if Mason and his people truly understood.

If Azrael was using the base, there would not be simple safeguards around it. The Enemy used unseen forces to protect their own. True, for outside appearance purposes there would be human guards and patrols, but beyond them would be the invisible, more dangerous sentinels: things like what they left behind in Mason's Tennessee home when they took Martin, and worse.

"I want you to check in every fifteen minutes," Mason said.

He smiled at the man. So, perhaps he did sense something of the real threat. "And if I miss once? You cannot afford to attempt a rescue."

Jaelon embraced him briefly. "Come back safely," she murmured to him.

"Such is my intent," he told her as firmly as he could manage.

Malthusan stuck out his hand and they gripped forearms for a long moment, eyes locked in silent accord. Populus broke off and bowed to Meeker.

"Until we meet again, my dear," he said, then looked at Mason. "Fifteen minutes," he told them, pulling the carrying strap over his head and seating it on his shoulder. Then, with a last look and smile, he left.

* * *

A huge project had developed under the sand in the vast wilderness of the Arabian Desert. Carved from the underlying rock by burrowing machines provided by Andlat Enterprises, a tunnel complex of unprecedented size stretched for miles like the web of some monstrous spider. Within its bowels a great army gestated, growing, training, waiting for the word to burst from its hidden womb and strike westward across the unsuspecting North African Bloc. Protected from discovery by its desert roof, the southern command of the Persian Empire strained against its bonds, anxious to begin its rampage across the nations that so innocently thought themselves immune from the terrors that swarmed over their neighbors across the Mediterranean. Only the delayed success of the Imperial forces in the north kept them at bay.

The North African Bloc had signed a non-aggression pact with the Empire and as long as they believed themselves safe, the nations of that bloc would ignore the desperate pleas for aid from their European counterparts. The Imperial commanders had learned from the past how disastrous trying to fight a war on two fronts could be. Patience, as trying as it was, was the key to victory; a lesson hard-learned and ignored at peril.

Within the European Bloc, cells like Mason's worked to undermine the Imperial gains or stop further advance. While conventional European forces fought with guns, bombs, tanks, and aircraft, the Army cells tracked and banished what Minions they could find. It soon became clear the Imperials were puppets of a central authority, a force working invisibly to provide logistical support and armament. That force sat apart from the combat, physically removed from danger of discovery by layers of false fronts and intermediary agents. Its inexhaustible resources poured into the ravenous Imperial coffers, its source as mysterious as the identity of the driving force behind the Imperial advance. The European cells struggled hopelessly against the phantom enemy.

And Dorian Azrael, safe in his anonymity, watched in amused satisfaction.

The opponent's efforts to track his involvement were amateurish, almost comical. The African campaign was nearly ready to launch. It remained only to move the troops across the borders of the client Arab states and stage them on the shores of the Red Sea. Neither that body of water nor the venerable Suez Canal would present much of an obstacle to his forces. The latest in sea and air transport would make short work of that, and any onshore defenders will have been nullified by sabotage, ambush, or bribery. He anticipated the fall of Cairo, Khartoum, and Addis Ababa within eight hours, Tripoli within twenty-four. By the end of the fifth day, Imperial forces would be occupying the Algerian Enclave all the way to the Senegal District. The North African Bloc's military acumen had never been that impressive, would be even less so now that his client companies controlled the communications and power grids. Without the ability to coordinate a defense, the African forces would fall like ripe wheat before the scythe. The entire continent would be under his control within a month.

After centuries of planning and decades of preparation, Azrael could almost taste the sweetness of victory. He would become the most powerful man in the world, dictating the actions of entire nations from the shadows, all for the glory of his master.

And his own pleasure, of course.

* * *

The terrain around the southern border of the base afforded plenty of cover right up to the perimeter. Populus knew that the outlying areas had been nearly bled dry of population since the rise of the megaplexes. Small villages like Mountain Home still existed, eking out a hard living from the increasingly wild surroundings. Game animals, all but hunted or crowded to extinction before, now roamed freely across their ancient habitats. He found this wonderful, somewhat like being back in the forests of his youth, the birdsong and aromas of pine and honeysuckle a reminder of the verdant scents that swept through his olive groves so long ago.

Following an animal trail, he made it to within 100 yards of the perimeter. There appeared to be little protection beyond an old-style cyclone fence topped by razor wire, not much of a challenge. He knew better. A few words of seeing revealed the wards hanging from the fence line. Another few words negated those weak wards easily. They were obviously not meant to thwart a determined, knowledgeable intruder, only to alert the guard of a breach from more mundane thieves. His cutting tool made short work of a large panel, opening it and sealing it behind him. Only a very close examination would reveal where the fence had been penetrated.

Inside the fence, cover was not so accessible. Luckily, the patrols were few and far between. Years of isolation had dulled the guard into a sense of routine security. He darted across a lane and behind a one-story structure, keeping to the shadows as much as he could. The unattended landscaping helped him remain concealed as he made his way deeper into the base, following the transponder signal. It might have been wiser to wait until dark to do this, but he had no way of knowing what kind of extra security might be scheduled for nightfall. Besides, in the daylight it was easier to see the patrol vehicles far off and gauge their true distance and direction than at night.

The signal led him to an oddly shaped building near the base's center. The frame that once held a sign identifying the building's purpose stood empty. He hesitated in the bushes covering the front of the edifice across the lane from it, watching for any traffic in or out.

An official-looking car pulled up and a woman and several uniformed men emerged from the building. They got into the car, which left in a hurry. After he was sure it was safe, he dashed across to the building and quickly examined its door. Amazingly, there was no lock or video surveillance to prevent him entering its lobby. He quietly slid inside, murmuring words of seeing and finding no resistance either mundane or esoteric. Whatever was in this building, its occupants obviously wanted to attract no attention nor reveal anything to the outside world.

The lobby was dark and the air reeked of dust and age. He found a main corridor running off toward the back of the building. A faded chart on one wall labeled "Fire Evacuation Plan" conveniently displayed the building layout. A glance at it told him there were only three rooms suitable for holding a prisoner. He took a moment to determine the best sites for the diversion charges, then headed deeper in.

Populus whispered more words of seeing to reveal any wards and gasped. Coiled in the center of the main corridor not more than ten feet away was an *apophis*, a serpent demon whose nature gave rise to an ancient Egyptian legend about the enemies of Ra. Invisible to normal sight, its scaled body glittered iridescently in the brightness of the seeing words.

Without his personal wards protecting him from detection by The Enemy agents, it would have already attacked, rendering him wounded in ways invisible to the eye but effectively paralyzing him physically, and rendering him easily captured.

He slipped past the *apophis* carefully, pausing briefly when the serpent raised its head and its forked tongue flit out toward him. He was fairly certain his personal wards were sufficient to prevent it detecting him, but a chill still went through him at its attention.

Finally, it settled back down with a sinuous move of its head and body that unfortunately planted its bulk directly between him and where he needed to go. He set his jaw and slowly pushed his way around it, squeezing as close to the wall as possible. Anyone unable to sense the *apophis* would think his actions odd, pressed hard against the corridor wall and sliding slowly against an invisible obstacle.

He planted the charges without encountering any other wards. It seemed strange that there should be only the one until he considered The Enemy probably thought it impossible anyone could have come this far unobserved.

The second room he searched for Martin was crowded with equipment. The transponder signal insisted his target was close by, and in a matter of seconds he found the hidden panel which opened the door to a concealed cell.

* * *

Maybe it was the waiting, maybe it was the weather, maybe it was just his fear for Janice, but he couldn't stand it any more. He went and found Mason lighting one of his damned cigars, watching the sky as if he was looking for something.

"We need to talk," he said.

Mason shook the match out and tucked the burnt stub into a pocket. He nodded. "Yes, I suppose we do."

"You let Nicholson go."

Mason sighed. "We've already discussed that. Going after him would have accomplished nothing and might have endangered everyone. Including Janice."

Overguard stiffened at the man's tone. It didn't matter whether he was right or wrong, he had no call talking down to him.

"You're the one endangering everyone," he retorted. "Nicholson learned all our strengths and weaknesses. He saw our faces. He listened to how we plan." He leaned toward Mason. "He even tried to get Janice to leave with him. What's more, I saw him talking with Populus, and now Populus is gone."

Mason scowled deeply. "Surely you don't think Populus..."

"I don't know what to think!" He paced a few steps away before turning back. "What happened to Chandler?"

Mason blinked. "Chandler?"

"David Chandler. Remember him? Hell, he was only in your cell for seven years!"

"Azrael had him killed," Mason said, grimly.

Overguard nodded. "And Martin?"

The other man flicked ash from the end of his cigar. He looked at the ash on the ground. "We all run risks."

"Not good enough!" he barked, pointing at Mason. "Not nearly good enough! We put our lives on the line..."

"We *all* do," Mason reminded him.

"...because you tell us to," he finished. "What do we get for it? What is it all for?"

Mason looked away, but didn't answer.

"What's it for, Mason?" he shouted.

"I don't know!" the other said forcibly.

The man's response stopped him cold. He had expected some platitude, some high-sounding excuse, not this.

"I really don't know," Mason repeated, facing him again. "I've asked myself that question a thousand times. You think I have no doubts? You think I don't want..." He stopped. "You think I haven't come close to walking away from it all myself?"

He passed a hand through his hair and sighed. "Maybe I've lived too long. Maybe I look like I don't care enough. I've been where you are a hundred times, Stephen. I watched friends and family die while I went on. I wandered from place to place looking for answers. I fought in wars where I came so close to death I could hear its wings, but it never came for me." He leaned against the van and took a long draw on his cigar. "It was never for me." Overguard at last heard sadness in his voice. After another moment, Mason looked at him. "If you want to take Janice and go, I understand. Truly, I understand."

Overguard stood quietly considering his words. Mason took his silence as a demand.

"I haven't found any answers yet," the Angelkiller said. "Once in a while I think I'm close, then something comes along and I'm right back where I was."

"Why go on, then?" he asked. "What's keeping you at this?"

Mason looked him in the eye and Overguard saw pain and sorrow in the man's face. The answer wasn't immediate, and maybe the man hadn't ever put it into words before.

"Because I have nothing else," Mason said.

Once again, the answer caught him unawares. His vision of the man as selfish and rash, unfeeling and unyielding, vanished. Mason was human after all. The anger and suspicion that had been plaguing him since Nicholson arrived melted away. He was sorry for what he said, harsh words to a fellow sufferer.

Vera Cruz changed him in ways he was only beginning to understand. It made him build walls against his own feelings, made him want to avoid commitment to anyone but himself. In a flash, he saw how it had affected Janice, making their relationship a series of uncomfortable encounters except for that one time in Haltwhistle when his walls had fallen away, when for a little while he forgot who he was and everything except her. In her arms, he became whole again.

He had something Mason didn't, and that gave him mixed feelings. He didn't know what to say. An apology rose up in him but refused to find voice. Looking at Mason, he knew it wasn't required. The man said he understood, and Overguard believed him.

Without another word, he walked away.

* * *

"There's the signal!" Overguard said as the monitor sounded its alarm.

Meeker rushed to the console to send the package. There

was a heart-stopping moment as the computers interacted. If Populus' metatoroidal virus ran into resistance, everything they'd done for the past several weeks would be in vain. They all watched tensely as the loading graphic bar filled.

The bar reached 77% and stopped. They watched nervously. Without Populus, there was no way to keep the Andlat computers from back-tracking to their location should the load abort. The virus input was supposed to be untraceable, but if something was intelligent enough to stop it, it would be intelligent enough to trace the hack to them.

The bar jumped to 91% and stopped again.

"Man, I wish Populus was here," Overguard breathed.

The bar moved again, hanging at 98% for an interminable second before "Upload Complete" appeared and they all could take a long-delayed breath.

"Thank God," Meeker said. "I thought for a minute there we'd..."

A raucous alarm cut her off. The monitor screen blinked once, blacked out, and all the computers went dead.

"That can't be good," Overguard observed in the sudden silence.

"What happened?" Meeker asked, holding up her hands from the console. "I didn't do that."

"They must have tracked the transmission," Mason said. "That means they may have a lock on our location. We have to move."

"What about Populus? We can't just leave him," Meeker objected.

"We do not have a choice," Jaelon said. "We are too close to the megaplex. Trackers are probably launching as we speak."

Mason hopped into the driver's seat and started the van.

"The equipment outside..." Meeker began.

"We don't have time to get it," Mason answered. "Hold on. I'm going to take us as far north as cover will allow."

The others grabbed for support as the van lurched to life.

"At least we know the virus got in," Meeker said as she held on to the back of Mason's seat.

"Keep that thought," Mason told her.

The van lumbered across an open field and dove into the forest to follow a firebreak headed northeast. The trail wound briefly eastward then turned north, paralleling the river.

"How far do you think we can get before they find us?" Jaelon asked. She had commandeered the passenger seat and was craning her neck to look overhead through the forest canopy.

"I guess that depends on how soon they get to where

we were," Mason said. "It won't take long after that. This van leaves a trail a blind man could follow."

"Shouldn't we ditch it, then?" Overguard asked.

Mason shook his head, jerked the wheel to negotiate a series of hairpin curves. "Not until we're far enough away to be sure that Populus is safe when he gets back. As soon as they see we abandoned the equipment, they'll assume we left together. If we can get..."

He slammed on the brakes. Ahead of them, the firebreak ended at the edge of a deep ravine. He pounded the wheel in frustration.

"I don't think even this thing can fly," Meeker noted, looking at the thirty-foot gap to the other side.

A crackling noise brought their attention back to the monitor. For a few seconds there was nothing but static, then a familiar face appeared.

"Septimus Vernus," Azrael said. "I salute your ingenuity."

"Can he see us?" Jaelon asked.

"No, but he doesn't have to," Mason responded.

"Your attempt to shut down my company almost worked," Azrael was saying with a smile. "Too bad. I would have enjoyed a little more cat and mouse..."

The Minion paused as someone off camera spoke

unintelligible words. Azrael barked back in the same language, then glared blackly into the camera before shutting off the transmission.

Meeker looked at Mason, confused. "What...?"

"I believe he was just advised that they can't stop the virus," Jaelon surmised.

"Which means Andlat is failing!" Overguard exulted.

"And the domino effect of the metatoroidal virus will cascade into all their systems within seconds," Mason said.

"So...we won?" Meeker asked.

"We've made it this far," Mason nodded. "Now comes the really hard part."

"What's that?"

Mason yanked the van around to head east along the ravine edge.

"Staying alive."

9

The shield shuddered as the pulse battered against it. Maachen grunted under the impact, staggering backward two steps and falling to one knee.

His enemy showed no signs of fatigue. Maachen wished he could say the same. His limbs ached horribly. The shield weighed a ton. He had bought only a brief reprieve from defeat by turning his attention to the woman. If anything, he thought, he'd only delayed the inevitable. The tip of his sword rose more slowly with each parry. The shield came to bear later to each defense.

An ugly smile spread across her face. She saw the weakness and perversely, instead of pressing her advantage, she pulled back.

"Why do you continue with this ridiculous course?" she asked, stepping closer with every other word. "You cannot win. Submit, and perhaps my master will spare your useless life."

"Never!" Maachen blurted.

Her smile widened unnaturally. "I hoped you would say that." She lifted both hands, weaving an intricate pattern that glowed in unnameable colors in the air.

Maachen tried to lift the shield, but its weight was too much for him. He braced himself for the final blow.

"I think you need to reconsider," Maachen heard from behind him.

He looked around at a man arrayed in esoteric garb. He had the appearance of the Mediterranean about him. The woman turned to the new threat, striking out. The newcomer brushed the pulse aside, unperturbed.

Snarling, she unleashed a barrage of attacks, gouts of power that rippled through the air between them, to spatter harmlessly against an unseen barrier hanging before the man.

"I have come for him," the man announced. "He is not for you."

"You have no authority here!" she shouted, preparing another onslaught.

"You have no idea what true authority is," the man replied. "Your kind lives in the self-deception that you are your own authority. Only the fearful recognize no one greater than themselves."

"Saccharine stupidity," she growled.

The man smiled mirthlessly at that. He went to Maachen and helped him to his feet.

"Courage, my friend," he told Maachen. "Your time has not come yet."

Maachen leaned against his sword, looking between the two. This seemed too easy. A savior appearing a just the right moment? Just as he was sure he had lost, just as he had despaired of any hope? Was this a trick? Some diabolical, sick joke at his expense? He eyed his rescuer closely.

"Who are you?" he asked.

"My name is Krato Populus," the man answered, smiling.

"Populus? You look... different."

The Greek Knight nodded. "I imagine so. My avatar would be affected by the interface software. It has to approximate my signal image based on its internal code."

"Well, you do talk like him." Only then did Maachen notice the woman had vanished.

"She left several seconds ago," Populus said to his unasked question.

A chill went through him. If she was gone, then what would she do... "My body. It's..."

"Not to worry. Your captors have much more to occupy their attention."

* * *

The global network that kept Andlat Enterprises alive was in its death throes.

Hundreds of IT experts worked frantically to stop the advance of whatever was destroying the system, but catching the virus was like trying to catch smoke in a sieve. It slipped by every firewall, every heuristic algorithm with supernatural ease. They began unplugging everything from the network in an attempt to isolate its source, but it was too late. The malware, whatever it was, had gone resident within nanoseconds into every computer's operating system.

Andlat Enterprises expired in spite of every effort. With it went all the guidance and intelligence infrastructure attached to the Persian Imperial forces.

The invasion of the European Bloc ground to a sudden halt. Command and control centers went down and refused to reboot. Front line troops lost contact, stalled in their advance. Without orders and coordination, the Imperial campaign was at an end. European Bloc armies, unencumbered by such a problem, began to push back.

The tide had turned.

* * *

Martin suddenly found himself back in the featureless room where his captors took him after his abduction from Mason's Tennessee house.

Gone was the strength in his legs, returned was the pain he'd nearly forgotten that held him in a wheelchair since the fire at his own home. He nearly passed out from the shock of the sudden transition, holding up with an effort.

"We must move quickly."

Through the haze of his pain, Martin realized Populus was unbinding him, disconnecting the I/O and helping him to his feet.

To his feet? He looked down in astonishment. He was standing! He wanted to know how it was possible, wanted to ask Populus what had happened, but the Knight was urging him toward the door.

The place was in an uproar. The banging of a fire alarm sounded almost deafeningly in the corridor and smoke obscured the passage. They stumbled toward the exit, Martin nearly blinded by the smoke, pushing down the cough he was afraid might betray them to The Enemy. He soon saw he needn't have worried. What few people who were in the building appeared to be more concerned with getting out than stopping them. After a little, he found he could not only stand but run on his newly-healed legs. That feeling, combined with everything else going on around them, set his heart pounding.

He nearly ran into Populus, who had stopped in the hallway and was looking around anxiously.

"What's wrong?" he asked. "We need to get out of here."

Populus hesitated only another second, then surged ahead. They melted into the fleeing crowd that spilled into the street, then ducked behind a nearby building as fire response crews screeched up and first responders ran in.

Quickly, they dashed toward the perimeter but brought up short when several patrols flashed by.

"This way," Populus said.

Darting from building to building, they made their way around the edge of the base, looking for a chink in the perimeter patrols. It soon became apparent the guard was on high alert.

"We're trapped," he said as they neared the airfield on the north side of the complex.

Populus grimaced. "It would appear so." He slapped his thigh in frustration. "We cannot remain hidden forever. They will soon discover it was a false alarm. When they find you are gone, they will rightly assume there are intruders on the base and begin to search."

"What do we do? Can we take out one of the patrols?"

"Not without betraying our position. My guess is they are all in comm contact. Any attempt to neutralize one patrol will bring one or more to their rescue."

There was the sound of flyers overhead. They hunched down and watched as three of the black machines flew by and landed. Six men piled out of each one.

"Search parties, no doubt," Populus said. "We do not have much time."

The new arrivals formed up briefly, then stomped away toward a large building nearby. The three flyer pilots appeared as the vehicles idled. Populus and Martin saw them speak together, then two followed the main troops. The Greek thumped him on the arm.

"Stay here," he commanded.

Martin nodded. It wasn't hard to guess what the man had in mind.

Populus vanished into some landscaping bushes. Martin watched tensely as his friend appeared on the other side of the flyer behind the lone guard and stealthily approached. The Knight came up behind the man and dealt one quick blow to the back of the pilot's neck. The man crumpled.

Martin sprang from cover and ran toward the flyer as Populus climbed in.

"Nicely done," he said. "Can you fly one of these things?"

"No, but I am sure the computer can." Populus scanned the controls, then looked at him. "Any ideas?"

He took in the onboard computer console. Yes, there might be something he could do. "I just need a minute," he said.

"Work on it. I will disable the others."

Martin started to object, but the Greek was already gone. He turned back to the controls.

"Okay," he said to himself. "It's just like driving an aircar, right?" The console blinked at him in a dazzling array of readouts and monitors. "Yeah, right."

* * *

Azrael's limousine pulled up to the main gate. The guard didn't come out to challenge them at once, engaged with his comm panel.

"What's the problem?" he asked the driver.

"I'm sorry, sir. I don't know."

The howl of a general alarm bellowed outside. The guard hurried from his post to the limo.

"Who the hell..." he started to say, then recognized the

insignia on the driver's shoulder. He snapped to attention. "Sorry, sir."

"What is happening?" Azrael demanded.

"We have an intruder on the base, sir."

"What?" Azrael pounded on the driver's seat. "Go!"

The limousine leapt forward, nearly knocking the guard down as he tried to jump clear. The car smashed through the guard bar, sending splinters flying.

Azrael cursed as he saw a flyer lift off in the distance and head west. He grabbed the comm unit and thumbed in the code for base command. He didn't wait for the person who answered to identify themselves.

"Track that flyer!"

* * *

Martin watched nervously as the river appeared below. They had gone west in the hopes it would fool any possible pursuers into believing they were crossing to the other side. Populus worked frantically at the controls as he watched for any sign they were being followed.

"I think we lost them," he said.

"Let us hope so," his friend said, hands busy at the controls.

His heart was still pounding, but he was beginning to feel better about their chances. It was lucky the pilot had left the engine idling. He wasn't sure how long it would have taken to get the flyer started. As it was, it turned out all he needed to do was plug in some lat-longs to convince the machine to help them escape. Populus had rushed back in and immediately taken over, leaving him to take up station as lookout.

"With the other flyers disabled, they will have to pursue in ground vehicles," Populus said. "Let us hope there are no more flyers on the way."

"What if they have aircars on the base?"

"We can outrun those." The Greek leaned back from the console. "The positioning monitors are disabled," he said with a sigh. "As long as we stay below radar, they can only track us by visual from satellites now."

"That'll only buy us a few minutes."

"I know." Populus fiddled with the controls again and they banked south. "We will be off their grid soon. They will have to do a wide scan to find us."

They flew along the riverbank just below treetop height. Martin tried not to flinch as the trees passed only a few feet away.

10

Azrael and his bodyguards stomped into the base command. The room, filled with monitors, comm consoles, computers, runners and workers noisily hustling about, instantly fell silent. It was a familiar reaction to his appearance before subordinates, especially those who had reason to believe they had incurred his displeasure.

A woman scurried forward. Azrael recognized her as Cora Drapacz, the interrogator assigned to Martin. He had her imported from Prague specifically for this assignment because of her record of success with similar cases. She was host to a minor Minion of his line.

She bowed slightly. "Welcome. You honor us."

Azrael ignored that. "Where is the prisoner?"

She shuffled uneasily.

"Speak!"

"He has escaped," she admitted, eyes downcast.

"The flyer," he supposed.

She nodded in another bow.

"You are tracking it."

There was a brief pause. "Yes."

Azrael narrowed his eyes at her. She was hiding something. She wilted under his stare.

"They have crossed the river," she revealed. "Our other flyers were sabotaged but are being repaired. The enemy has disabled their positioning monitor, but we are re-tasking a satellite for a grid search."

"So, you don't know where they are."

She took a hesitant breath. "Not exactly."

"Do I need to remind you what will happen if they are not found?"

He was satisfied to see her eyes widen in fear as she shuddered.

"No, sir."

He looked around at the rest of the people in the room. The base personnel were properly cowed, so there was no problem other than this escape to handle. As yet, none of them had worked out a way to maneuver this into personal advantage, but if he was still to use Martin to his own, he needed to move quickly.

"I have a call to make," he told them. "I require an interface."

She motioned toward a nearby console. The worker at the station stood and offered his seat. He swung into it and thumbed the communications open to the right frequency.

* * *

The computers in the van sparkled to life again. Mason pulled the vehicle to a stop under some oak trees and turned to find Azrael's face peering at them from the monitors.

"Septimus Vernus," the Minion was saying, "you might like to know your rescue attempt has failed. If you want to see your friends again, meet me at the following coordinates in four hours." Azrael's face gave way to a numerical readout, which remained onscreen as he spoke again. "Four hours."

The screen went blank.

"Did we get that?" he asked.

"Yes," Jaelon said, inputting the data to the positioning system. "We can be there in three hours depending on terrain."

"Then we have a little time to plan," he said.

"It's an obvious trap," Overguard stated. "We don't even know if they're alive."

"True," Jaelon allowed. "However, we must not assume they are dead either."

"Dead or alive, he can use them against us," Malthusan said.

Mason stared at him in growing alarm. What was the Cypriot saying? He had heard rumors in the past about Minions using the dead, tales that stretched back centuries. Was Malthusan saying what he thought? He looked at the others and all but Jaelon seemed to be thinking the same thing. Malthusan shrugged.

"Until we are certain it is hopeless, we must consider their rescue. This he knows. We have no choice."

There was a general sigh of relief, or at least Mason thought he heard it. For a terrible moment, he'd thought...

"We should get started now anyway," Meeker said. "We don't know what obstacles there are between here and there. We might need the extra time."

Mason agreed and pulled the van back out the the trees. He set off in the southeasterly direction the positioning system suggested.

"Won't this take us close to the airbase?" Overguard worried.

"It can't be helped," Mason replied. "The forest is too

thick to the north to travel in a van this size."

"Just exactly how close to the base does he want us to meet?"

Jaelon checked. "About two and one half miles north-northwest."

"Nearly spitting distance," the Texan said glumly.

"Indeed," Jaelon said. "But what else can we do?"

Overguard shook his head and kept silent. The landscape flowed by them in a steady parade of oak, hickory, poplar, and gum. The occasional honeysuckle vine or mimosa tree might have brightened their trip any other time. As it was, no one was in the mood to enjoy the view.

* * *

Azrael snapped off the comm unit. The resistance in Europe had stalled his plans through such maneuvers. He wasn't going to allow it to happen here. Once Europe and Africa were subjugated, he wanted the Americas to be ready for invasion. He had underestimated the resistance before, but no more.

"They have been an obstacle long enough. It is time they were put down," he said, almost to himself. He looked at one of the bodyguards. "Stay here. Coordinate the death squads while I handle this. I want all North American resistance neutralized.

I don't care what has to be done. Whether you have to take out one man or a thousand, do it!" As the man nodded his acknowledgment, he turned to Drapacz. "You will come with me. I will teach you how to deal with these people."

She bowed. "As you wish."

* * *

The van pitched over the uneven ground, a constant irritant that made it hard for Meeker to think.

They all sensed they were headed into something that was going to be different, something none of them except maybe Mason had faced before. She doubted even Jaelon and Malthusan had experienced a similar confrontation. This was no small-time criminal they were going up against. It wasn't a corporate raider like Andrew, not even a Minion like Azazel. This was one of The Enemy's most important and successful lieutenants. He might not be the Angel of Death, but everything they knew about Dorian Azrael said he would be almost as fearsome to oppose.

She was suddenly very glad of the others' presence. She didn't know if she would have the courage to go along without them at her side. She looked at Jaelon and Mason up front, their faces almost mirror images of determination and alertness.

It was amazing how alike they were, and yet how different. Malthusan sat strapped into the bench seat on the other side of the van, head down, apparently and unbelievably napping. The man's nerves must be stronger than steel.

Stephen sat beside her. He took her hand.

"Okay?" he asked.

She nodded mutely.

"Don't worry, I got you," he swore.

She managed a grateful smile.

It was going to be a long three hours.

* * *

They pulled the van to a stop near the clearing. Azrael's limo was already there, a low dark shadow in the gathering gloom.

"Stay here," Mason told the others.

"No way!" Overguard snapped. "You're not going anywhere alone."

"Stephen's right," Meeker interjected. "Azrael's not to be trusted. We're all going."

Jaelon and Malthusan nodded their agreement. For a moment, he started to object, but decided otherwise. The Knights were sent to help, after all. He had no objection to their accompanying him, but as for the others, that was a different story. Overguard and Meeker were just starting a new life, one that deserved a chance to succeed. They shouldn't be jeopardizing that. Still, looking at their faces, he knew that they would never agree to a direct order to stay.

"All right," he said. "Jaelon, Malthusan, huddle up. We need to work out a plan. Janice and Stephen, see if you can find something in here we can use against Azrael that can do more than stun him."

"Right," Meeker and Overguard chimed. They headed to the back of the van.

Mason motioned to the Knights, who nodded silently. The three of them slipped out quietly and began making their way under cover of the trees toward the clearing.

* * *

Meeker searched for only a few moments before realizing none of the weapons in the van had the kind of power they needed. The best she could find was a slug thrower that might knock him over, maybe render him unconscious. She turned to find Overguard leaning over her shoulder. She looked past him.

The others were gone.

"Stephen...?"

He followed her gaze, then muttered something under his

breath and ran to the front of the van. She brought up beside him. They could see Mason and the Knights darting from tree to tree, approaching the clearing. They could also see two heavily armed men leave the limo and disappear into the cover near the vehicle. A woman came out of the back of the limo, stood beside it, and faced the direction Mason and the others were.

"This isn't good," she said. "They know."

"It *was* a trap," Overguard said, gritting his teeth. "And they're walking right into it."

"We have to warn them!"

Overguard looked around for a moment, then looked at her. His face was tense, but the question it asked was all too obvious. Desperate action was needed and he wanted to know if she was up to it.

Everything she'd experienced with the cell flashed before her eyes. From the time she met Stephen, she had become part of something greater than herself. She had become a different person from the student who sat gossiping in the coffee house in Amsterdam. A better person, she hoped. Someone willing to do what was necessary when it was necessary. She'd seen Martin and Populus put everything on the line for this. Was she at least as courageous as they? Could she find it within herself to act now, without another thought for herself? It was a simple yes or no question. That's what it all boiled down to.

Silently, she nodded.

He slid into the driver's seat. He cranked the engine. "Hang on!" he shouted and hit the throttle.

The van growled, leapt forward, tearing its way through the underbrush, careened off a tree he couldn't avoid, and burst into the clearing with a roar. He aimed the van at the limo. Meeker had just enough time to brace herself before the impact.

There was a loud noise, disorientation as the van spun under her, a scream of metal rending. She felt herself hurled forward. Something collided with her going the other way. The world got blurry and unreal. Her ears rang from the cacophony inside and out. Equipment shaken loose whirled about her, or was she falling?

Then everything went very still and quiet.

* * *

Mason watched in horror as the van sped into the clearing and smashed into the limo. The woman standing beside it, paralyzed by the sight of the oncoming vehicle, didn't have time to dodge. She was consumed in the crash, vanishing without a sound.

Forgetting stealth, Mason and the others ran toward the wreckage, skidding to a stop only when they saw Azrael climb, incredibly unhurt, from the remains of his vehicle.

The van had got the better of the crash but lay on its side, smoking from some unseen injury. Mason started toward it, then hit the ground at the sound of gunfire. The shooters were hidden in the brush either side of the clearing, pinning him down each time he tried to move. They must have been given orders not to kill him. They couldn't have missed at such short range.

The echoes of the crash and gunshots died away, leaving him to wonder what to do. One or both of his friends were in that van. Were they hurt? Were they alive?

"Mason!" he heard Azrael shout. "Come out, Mason. My men won't shoot."

He turned to Jaelon and Malthusan, crouched in the high grass nearby. They returned his look expectantly. It was clear they were waiting for his decision. He had no doubt they would follow his lead, but for the first time in years he found he couldn't move.

It wasn't that he feared for his life. That fear left him long ago, the effect of centuries on the front lines. After seeing how fleeting life could truly be, he found the idea of his own mortality held little terror.

It wasn't that he was afraid of facing Azrael. He had faced

Minions before. Azrael was just another one after all, no matter how powerful.

It was a premonition of an end and a beginning, a dread he hadn't felt since before Sorius recruited him in the blood-soaked battlefield on the coast of Picentia. It was the same fear and uncertainty he felt when Sorius first asked him to follow the Celtiberian priest off that crimson-tainted ground into a mystery beyond his comprehension. It was a hesitation on a precipice between a world of the familiar, unpleasant and trying as it was, and an abyss of the unknown whose depth and breadth stretched before him as a yawning chasm of uncertain nature.

This was why the Knights had come. For this moment, for this decision. Every move he'd made in his life, everything he'd experienced, every battle fought, had been preliminary to this.

"Septimus Vernus!" the Minion shouted, the evocation of his birth name setting his personal wards aquiver. "Come out and face me!"

He steeled himself against the paralysis, forcing his reluctant limbs into motion. He sensed the Knights moving off to cover him as he stood up. They would deal with Azrael's lackeys, but the final confrontation was his and his alone.

It came to him that always before he'd battled a Minion

he'd depended on the support of his comrades to bolster his courage. The loyalty of Tripp, the steadfastness of Martin, the courage of Meeker and Overguard, had filled the unrealized failings of his own frailties. His sense of duty may have driven him to this, but now even that seemed insufficient.

He was laid bare to himself, aware at last of how he'd used the others unfairly to do what he should have done himself. At that moment, he hated who he had become: selfish and self-centered, excusing his own cowardice under the guise of leadership. Who was he to believe he had the authority to determine another's fate? He was only a man after all, the thought echoed in his mind, the one he had used as an excuse too long.

He took a step toward Azrael.

And nearly stumbled when he saw Overguard clamber out of the van's wreckage, bloodied and dazed, Meeker following almost immediately.

Relief washed over him as he saw the Knight's van had protected them from being killed in that horrible crash. The miraculous vehicle had saved their lives for the moment, but Azrael had noticed them. The Minion looked from them to Mason and a feral grin spread over his features.

"Did you know, Vernus," he said, raising a hand toward

them, "that the human body is capable of some incredible things? Have you ever heard of psychokinesis?"

Mason stood, uncertain what to do. Azrael was closer to them than he was. If he tried to charge, were they strong enough to defend themselves?

"Azrael!" he yelled. "This is just between us. Leave them out of this."

The Minion's laugh cut him cold. "Just between us? Apparently not! They tried to kill me, Vernus. I'm just defending myself."

Mason watched as Meeker lifted what looked like a weapon and pointed it at Azrael. She must have found it in the van, but all the Knights' weapons were designed to stun or incapacitate, not kill. Surely it wouldn't have much effect on Azrael. Couldn't she see that?

"No, Janice!" he shouted.

Azrael waved his right hand in her direction. Whatever he intended to strike her never reached her. Overguard threw himself between them and took the full force. Both he and Meeker flew backwards over the smoking van and out of sight.

Mason's heart dropped. Azrael turned to face him again, the grin on the human visage betraying a demonic power.

"Where are your friends, Vernus? The Pictish girl and the

big Cypriot?" He looked around. "I know you're there, lurking like cowards. Come out and play."

Mason began slowly walking toward the Minion. He hesitated when the limo burst into flame behind Azrael, framing the man in an infernal glow. The smoke from the van poured into the clearing, making his eyes smart and sticking in his throat. The smell of burning fuel, oil, and flesh threatened his stomach. Azrael looked unaffected, almost comfortable.

"Reminds me of home," the Minion said, as if reading his thoughts.

"It's over, Azrael," Mason said around a cough. "The war is lost. Andlat Enterprises is done. You're beaten."

Azrael laughed. "A minor setback. You're a fool if you think it's anything more than that."

"I know it is more than that, just as I know you are afraid to admit it."

"You think so?" Azrael shot a hand at him.

Mason felt like he'd been hit by a thunderbolt. His own wards took some of the impact, but as it was he flew backward to land hard, ears ringing, vision blurred. He levered himself up to a sitting position and shook his head, trying to focus. He thought he felt a hand on his shoulder, heard Jaelon's voice inside his head.

"Be strong, Vernus," she said, and this time his personal wards sang. He felt a warmth spread into his chest from her touch, a healing warmth that penetrated deeper than flesh. He pulled himself upright.

His body ached from the blow. It wanted rest. He ignored its plea, moved two steps closer to Azrael. The Minion was a dark silhouette against the glare of the burning vehicle.

"I shall enjoy killing you, Vernus," Azrael said, his voice as much an animal growl as human. "I allowed you to live too long."

"You're lying. You allowed nothing," Mason croaked through the dryness. "You're not in control. You never have been. You are merely a tool of your master."

Azrael replied as before, and Mason flew backward again to slam into the ground. He gasped, trying to recover the wind knocked out of him. He forced himself to struggle back up, drawing on that warm healing that still tingled inside. He could feel his wards weakening. How much longer could their armor protect him?

"I never took you for a masochist, Vernus," Azrael said. "Are you really enjoying this so much?"

Mason doggedly pushed forward through his pain, determined to reach the Minion. He had no illusion he might do anything but try to subdue Azrael, but more than anything else he needed to prove to himself that he could face down his own doubts whatever happened.

"Spare yourself further suffering," Azrael said, a mock concern in his tone. "Look around. Your friends are just watching this go on. They have abandoned you. So has your master, Angelkiller. What kind of friend is He to allow *this*?" The Minion punctuated the last word by snapping both hands toward him.

The agony nearly made him black out. He felt the impact as a massive, crushing blow from neck to groin as his wards failed. Spots swam before his eyes as he lie looking into the darkening heavens, a few stars gazing uncaring at him from their inaccessible height. Each breath was an agonizing effort through broken ribs. He coughed, tasted blood.

"Had enough, Angelkiller?" Azrael taunted.

Mason was tempted to say yes. How easy it would be to just lie there, to surrender without further resistance. Had he stood enough against Azrael? What would be his reward? Another strike would finish him. Then who would lead his cell...

But then, there was no one left to lead. They were all gone. Chandler, dead. Martin and Populus, disappeared. Overguard and Meeker killed. There was no one else to look after. Only himself.

He would mourn them, yes. Afterward, if he survived this, he would take the time to deal with the guilt and remorse, but for right now the soldier took over. It was a simple matter of survival. No complications, no distractions. His mind cleared, the clarity of combat. He was free, free of care for the others, free of care for his own life. Nothing mattered but putting Azrael down, showing the Minion what it meant to be willing to set everything aside but service to the Master. Azrael might never understand it, might never grasp that idea of loyalty and fidelity to a cause, but Mason knew it now in a way which had evaded him. With that realization, the responsibility he'd felt for so long fell away from him like a heavy chain that had bound him for years. That freedom even made it somehow easier to breathe. With it came strength enough to again get to his feet.

"Back for more?" Azrael goaded. "Having fun? I know I am." He motioned an invitation for Mason to come closer. "I suppose I should thank you for the entertainment. I admit, I never expected you to last this long. I can almost understand how you've survived all these years."

Mason set his teeth and continued forward a step, two, three. He was only thirty feet from the Minion now. Azrael was nodding at him.

"That's right. Just a little farther now," he coaxed. "Your friends are finally showing signs of concern. I think your courage may be shaming them into doing something rash."

"Mason, stop!" Jaelon shouted.

"Yes, stop," Azrael mimicked. "Oh, dear, don't go near the terrible man!"

Mason ignored them, continuing forward. Twenty feet. Azrael appeared to have forgotten him. Fine, he thought, and took another step.

"Surrender and vacate, Azrael," Jaelon commanded. "Your time is over. You must answer for what you have done."

"What I've done?" the Minion responded. Almost casually, he motioned at Mason. "Stay!"

Mason found himself unable to move. He strained against the paralysis in increasing frustration. Azrael was almost within his reach. Even his tongue refused to obey. He couldn't voice his dismay as Azrael turned his full attention to Jaelon.

"What I've done, my dear, is build an empire from nothing. What have you done? What have you accomplished for your Master?"

"Surrender and vacate," Jaelon repeated. Mason couldn't see her, but from Azrael's attitude it looked as if she, too, was approaching.

"Surrender? To whom? You and your bodyguard there?" Azrael shook his head sadly. "Not likely. You see, I'm not done yet. You may have broken Andlat Enterprises, but you have no idea just how far my power extends. I have resources I haven't even touched. People who owe me. People loyal only to me."

"For the last time, surrender and vacate!"

"Or what?" Azrael scoffed.

Mason heard Jaelon and Malthusan's voices in concert uttering words he remembered from the night they'd exorcised Azazel from Michael Jenkins. There had been three Knights then, working together. Would the same ceremony work against Azrael? Would the strength of two suffice?

Whatever the possibility might be, it distracted the Minion from him. The paralysis dropped away. He charged Azrael as he felt the attack aimed at the Knights thrum in the air beside him.

11

Populus and Martin arrived at the campsite to find the place empty except for the abandoned satellite equipment. Their initial alarm faded as it became apparent the others had left unpursued.

"Where are they?" Martin asked, scanning the area.

Populus shrugged and considered for a moment. They wouldn't have abandoned the camp needlessly. Something must have forced them to move, but what? There was only one possibility he could think of.

"The virus signal," he said. "It must have gone wrong. They would have left to keep from being caught. Wherever they are, we have to hope they are up to the task." He clapped Martin on the back. "Have faith, my friend. We can track their progress from the air."

Martin glanced nervously around and overhead. "Looks

like they went toward the base. Is it safe for us to basically head back the way we came?"

"Safe or not, we have to follow." He thought quickly. "You go back to the flyer. I will be right there. I have to get something, if it is still here."

It was. He snatched the little device off the satellite dish console and sprinted for the flyer. Fitted into the vehicle's comm, he could decrypt any scrambled transmissions and stay one step ahead of Azrael's assigned pursuers.

He climbed in behind Martin and they set off along the van's track.

* * *

Mason dragged himself back into consciousness. He didn't remember going down, but he hurt all over. The world was fuzzy, with a crimson tinge. Overguard's body lay a few feet away, the man's eyes open, vacant, accusing. He looked away only to catch sight of Malthusan's unmoving bulk.

"Get up," Azrael growled.

Leaning his head back to gaze at the bright stars, Mason sighed. He should have known they had little chance against Azrael. The Minion might not truly be the Angel of Death, but he could be just as dangerous.

"Get up!"

Mason levered his body up, staggering a little, fighting dizziness.

"You should have been satisfied taking out Azazel, Mason. You and your friends would have lived longer." The Minion grinned at him. "I must admit, though, you have been more successful than anyone else of your kind at being a thorn in my side."

"Happy to have been of service," Mason croaked. He tasted blood, spat. "You should know we've taken down your arms dealers and the people you placed in the Imperial forces are being arrested as we speak."

Azrael laughed. "Of course I know. You think I'm a fool? I found out about your interference weeks ago."

"You...?" Mason choked, confused.

"My organization gets unwieldy after a few years," Azrael went on. "Success attracts the ambitious and corrupt. It's amazing how efficient and motivated they can be. Even so, after a while they have to be removed... culled, if you will. Otherwise you can lose control of the big picture." Azrael tilted his head at Mason. "Haven't you learned that yet? Isn't that what your Master does? Keep the most ambitious, the most effective around until they know too much, then sacrifice them to the enemy while He recruits? Isn't that why you're here? To die in His service?"

"Do not be deceived by his argument," Mason heard from behind him. Jaelon's voice reflected her pain, but her tone carried defiance.

"My dear Jaelon," Azrael said, "I believe you of all people should know how He works. After all, wasn't it Clement who said the Conflict was not worth the death and destruction? Wasn't it he who asked you to abandon the eternal bloodshed and spend your life with him at that little farmhouse?"

"Your words do not hurt me, demon," Jaelon retorted. "Do you think you are the first to tempt me so?" She chuckled, then coughed. "Truly, your kind knows nothing of real love and faith."

Azrael grunted, annoyed. "I have no time to debate philosophy with you. There are other, more pressing matters that require my attention." He pointed at Mason. "Say hello to your Master from us, Vernus. I'm sure he'll remember our names." He showed his teeth in a mirthless grimace. "Legion."

Mason heard the report and saw the bright flash. He had a moment to wonder at how loud the shot had been before he was thrown backward by the impact and blackness closed down around him.

* * *

Janice Meeker blinked grit out of her eyes and struggled up to lean against the side of the van. Her head throbbed and there was a copper taste in her mouth. There was something in her hands. She looked down at the slug-thrower and it took a second for her to recognize it.

"Your words do not hurt me, demon," she heard Jaelon say. "Do you think you are the first to tempt me so? Truly, your kind knows nothing of real love and faith."

"I have no time to debate philosophy with you. There are other, more pressing matters that require my attention," Azrael growled. He looked at Mason. "Say hello to your Master from us, Vernus. I'm sure he'll remember our names. Legion."

As Azrael pointed at Mason, Janice lifted the end of the weapon toward him. Totally engrossed in dealing with Mason and the Knight, he didn't notice her as she aimed. It toned its readiness. She pulled the trigger.

There was a bright flash and a roar. Azrael flew back into the burning limousine, his body catching fire from the flaming fuel. An unearthly howl sounded from his flailing form, then it was still.

Her eyes smarting from the smoke filling the clearing, she

squinted nervously toward the flames. Was Azrael dead? No, of course not. You couldn't kill a Minion. But he had been in a mortal form, Dorian Azrael's body. She could see it burning, smell the flesh as it popped and sizzled.

Timidly, she stepped from the cover of the van. Her foot bumped something hidden in the heavy smoke lying thick on the ground. She knelt to look at it.

Stephen's eyes were still open, but there was no life in them. She stared at the body and choked back a sob. How had it come to this? Now that it had actually happened, she realized she never truly understood the Conflict; its cost, its demands on those who fought.

The weapon was suddenly very heavy. She let it fall and stepped back from it as she would from a poisonous serpent.

"Janice," she heard Jaelon say.

She hurried to the Knight. Malthusan's lifeless body was draped across her protectively. Jaelon's legs were bloodied and bent oddly, but her eyes were bright. With an effort, Meeker managed to roll the big Knight's bulk off her, trying not to think about the awful way the body flopped limply.

"I'm sorry," Meeker cried. "I didn't know what else to do. He was going to kill Mason."

"Hush, girl!" Jaelon smiled. "You did rightly. You saved

Mason and yourself."

Meeker found herself shaking. She tried to stop, but it only made it worse.

"Do not resist what you feel," Jaelon said. "It is what makes us different from The Enemy – conscience." She motioned weakly for Meeker to come closer, took her hand. In a voice that faded a little with each word, she went on. "Remember, you did what had to be done. You did what was right."

Meeker gasped as the woman's hand slipped from her own and the Knight's eyes closed.

"Jaelon?" She shook the woman but there was no response. "Jaelon!" She nearly cried with relief when the Knight's eyelids fluttered and she turned her head.

A groan from nearby brought her around. Mason sat up, rubbing dirt and blood from his eyes. She looked back at Jaelon, touched the Knight's face, and anger rose in her. Stephen and Malthusan had paid the ultimate price. Jaelon was maimed, maybe mortally wounded. Martin, gone. Populus, missing. Andrew had turned on them. All that, but Mason just went on and on? Why him? What made him so special?

She looked at Stephen's broken body, at the Knights lying unmoving, and the heat in her overflowed. She charged Mason, shrieking her frustration and hurt. He threw up his arms to fend off her attack but made no other effort to prevent her. For long moments, she pounded on him, cursing him and wishing him dead. He stoically endured her onslaught without a word, raising his defenses only when she began to tire.

Finally, she collapsed to her knees, allowing the tears to take over. Her anger had broken, leaving her nothing but despair and grief. She despaired of what would happen to her. She grieved Stephen. Her life, once full and exciting, had become dark and horrible.

This was what The Enemy did, she thought. Azrael might be gone, but he'd left his mark behind.

She felt a hand on her shoulder and looked into Mason's battered visage.

"Help me with Jaelon?" he asked.

They looked around as the ground rumbled under them. Mason picked her up and pushed her toward the other woman.

"Get her to cover," he commanded. "Go! Now!"

* * *

Mason mumbled the words to bolster his personal wards. They might not handle what was coming, but he wasn't going to give up without a fight.

The rumbling increased, accompanied by a shaking of

the ground under his feet. He moved to put himself between Meeker and whatever it was that was rising from the wreckage of the burning limousine.

A great shadow emerged in defiance of the flames' natural illumination, muting the crimson and yellow into blood and gore. It rose slowly, ponderously, as if only remembering how to move after centuries of inactivity. Seconds passed as it whirled, formless and obscene, to finally coalesce into a vaguely humanoid figure.

Mason dared a glance backward and was relieved to see Meeker had managed to drag Jaelon into the cover of the tree line. Only he and the apparition moved in the clearing now. The smoke and haze had settled to hang in an ankle-deep carpet over the windless meadow. Not a breath stirred its substance. Here and there the head of a dandelion poked through its gray, like alien trees on a bleak and desolate landscape. The smoking hulk of the van was a black silhouette against the limo's burning frame, but the shadow's darkness was ten times as black. It was as if the starless void of intergalactic space had settled before him, an emptiness whose depths his mind refused to plumb, preferring to reject rather than comprehend its truth.

"So, Vernus," a voice crawled out of that abyss to assault him deep inside. "So, you have taught her to kill."

He bit back a retort and fought growing nausea. The filthy wave of hatred and rage the voice rode into his mind made him gag. Colors, indescribable in their putrescent ugliness, accompanied those words, blighting his vision.

"Are you proud of what she's become?" the Minion asked. "She and her lover?"

"There is no reason for you to stay," Mason shouted. Why, he didn't know. The thing that had inhabited Dorian Azrael's body could certainly have understood had he but thought the words.

"Oh, but there is," it countered. "The law says I can."

"What law?"

"...*thine eye shall not pity; life for life, eye for eye, tooth for tooth, hand for hand, foot for foot...*"

"That's not your law. You can't tell me you recognize any of that."

The Minion's mirth echoed in him. Somewhere it touched the real world around him. The trees on the edge of the clearing shuddered and the smoky carpet under him whipped into tiny whirlpools as the ground trembled.

"You're right, Angelkiller. I don't. But you and your kind do. So, what are you going to do about it?"

"Do?"

"Your people killed my assistant, and then killed Dorian. Where is your sense of justice, Vernus? Where is your moral outrage?"

"It was self-defense!"

"Words," the Minion scoffed. "Excuses. Rationalizations."

He couldn't let himself be drawn further into this argument. Had the shadow moved closer without him noticing? What would happen when it reached him? He knew there was no use in running. Whatever came about was inevitable.

"I'm waiting, Vernus. Are you looking for the right words, or have you finally understood that your life is built on a fraud?"

The shadow was either getting larger or getting closer. He couldn't tell. The nausea was overwhelming. He dropped to his knees and vomited, but it didn't subside.

"It's all a lie, Vernus. Your cause, your life, all of it. A lie within a lie."

The physical pain from the beating he'd taken was forgotten. In its place was an abysmal, nameless ache. It wasn't merely fear. It was an agonizing despair, an open, festering wound filled with grief, remorse, regret, and recrimination.

So, this was what it was like to remember it all at once. All the mistakes. All the half-truths and deceptions he had to use to protect his identity through the centuries bloomed like funereal wreaths within him, the stench of their rotten aroma more a mental torture than he thought he could bear.

Was this what Jenkins felt when the Seraph appeared? Faced with his own failings, his own inadequacies, had he buckled under their weight?

Was this what judgment truly felt like? He vented a voiceless cry, unwilling to allow the Minion the satisfaction of knowing his pain, but unable to stop his need to protest his nakedness before that judgment.

* * *

Jaelon felt faint. The world around her blurred on the edges. Her legs were broken in several places, a result of the impact of Malthusan's body when Azrael attacked. The thought of her friend's death pierced through her pain. She could hear Mason arguing with someone, but all she saw was a shadow against the flaming limo.

It had to be the Minion. Free of Dorian, it should have gone back to its master. Why was it still there?

A ripple of power struck her wards as she felt Mason cry out. Hope surged in her as she recognized its source. She summoned what strength she could to sit up.

"Stay down!" Meeker whispered, the fear plain in her voice.

"We have to help."

"He said to keep you safe," the girl argued.

"There's no time. Give me your hand and close your eyes."

Meeker looked puzzled, but nodded and complied.

"Whatever you hear, do not open your eyes. Understand?"

"Y...Yes," Meeker stammered.

Jaelon reached out to that source, the nascent portion of Mason that had been the reason she and the other Knights were sent. He was almost there. He was waking.

She had almost despaired he would come to this. They had been sent not just to help the cell against Azrael, but to encourage within Vernus that spark, that tiny light he had sublimated so long. The potential had been there since his time with Sorius, but when the priest died Vernus' confidence in himself and his place had died as well. In spite of the several times he had been at the brink of rediscovery, in Italy and Acre and Roxbury and Nevada, he'd never taken the last step, never allowed himself the freedom to make that last decision. The Master wanted Vernus to break through that doubt, to find himself and become what he should have been so long ago.

She pushed with all her might at that last piece of resistance, finally felt it fall away at last. The question he'd never dared ask himself, the last chain that held him back, was released.

She had done all she could. The rest was up to him. All the pieces were there. Could he put them all together in time?

Exhausted, she lapsed into unconsciousness.

* * *

The shadow was almost upon him now. Its emptiness was pulling the warmth from him to fill its need. He could feel it feeding on his own emptiness; hungry, insatiable.

"Life for a life..."

A question lit up in him. Where it came from, he couldn't say. Perhaps it had been there all along, waiting for the right moment to break through, the moment when all his resistance to it was exhausted.

"Why?" he croaked, coughing.

The shadow paused. Maybe something in how that question was formed confused even the Minion. The rest of it poured from him, all inhibition gone, the dam broken.

"Why are you doing this?"

There was no conditional sense to the question. There was no target to it. The question might as well have been asked of him as of the Minion. What it asked was not about actions bound by time or place. Mason knew that as soon as the words were uttered. He also knew that, intertwined within those five words was a name, the true name of the Minion that hovered inches from his face. The pronunciation of those syllables with their subliminal message both conjured and commanded. The Minion could not refuse to answer. It could struggle, it could try to resist, but it could not refuse. It was a question he would have to answer for himself at some time in the future, but one the Minion must reply to now.

"Because He lied!" came the response in a plaintive cry of pain and anguish. "He promised us dominion over all things, then he created Men and took it away. He lied!" The cry was filled with the pain born of perceived betrayal, the sound of a weeping child, the wail of a soul bereft of its most precious treasure. "He gave Men what He promised to *us*!"

The nausea abated a little as the Minion grieved. Mason's mind cleared enough he could think through his own pain.

"Did He?" he challenged. "Who rules this world? Who runs the governments? The corporations? The armies?"

The shadow retreated almost imperceptibly. Mason sensed the beginnings of confusion. He pressed the wedge further.

"Isn't it *your* kind that controls this world? Isn't it your kind that have made it what it is?"

"We..."

"You say He lied, that He took dominion from you, but

who really has the control? Tell me!"

"Silence! You have no idea..."

"Your kind controls this world. Your kind has done so since the beginning. So, He didn't lie, did He?"

There was a silence so profound it was as if the world had stopped to take a breath.

"Did He?" Mason shouted into the sudden quiet. The compulsion in those words was nearly visible.

"No!"

The word was quick, pained, loud.

And it was more than just an answer to a question.

There was one thing no Minion was allowed. They could squabble and bicker amongst themselves. They could wage war on each other, cheat and steal and commit whatever atrocities they wished between themselves. All of that was allowed, even encouraged. There was only one thing they were not allowed, could never be allowed.

Doubt of their own Master's truth.

Faced with Mason's words, the Minion had entertained doubt.

It was brief, fleeting, a passing thought barely recognized, but it was enough to catch the attention of the Dark, for the briefest of sparks in utter darkness lights a multitude of details, things that cannot long endure the light of discovery. The memory of that spark might be the seed that could grow into revelation of that which the Dark wanted kept hidden, a knowledge whose roots could stretch out and undercut the carefully crafted and delicately balanced facade that was control of the world.

There could be only one response.

The very air around them darkened, thickening with a heavy scent of lilac grown putrid with age. The gray haze deepened, swelling into the surrounding atmosphere, sending grit into Mason's eyes and nose. Half-blind, he staggered to his feet and coughed against the dust trying to lodge in his throat as it flew before a sudden wind swirling around them both. He put up his arms to fend off the stinging dirt and stumbled backward. After several steps, he found he could gasp relatively fresh air. He rubbed tearing eyes, trying to clear the sand, panicked that the shadow might attack while he was disabled.

He was suddenly bombarded by a thunderous roar, a sound that reverberated in his chest and actually made his heart skip a beat. He forced his eyes open against the hurting, but could only make out vague outlines in the holocaust exploding over the crash site.

It was no longer just one shadow moving in the flames and smoke. He couldn't be sure how many there were, but the

Minion was no longer alone. Perhaps it was better he couldn't see properly. The part of him that was the source of his personal wards rang loudly, as they did in the presence of the unseen, only the alarm it blared this time was far stronger than anything he'd experienced before.

And there was a terror he couldn't describe; so intense, so all-encompassing, so overpowering that it drove him to the ground. He wanted to crawl away and hide forever. He wanted to burrow into the earth, pull it in behind him so that he could never be seen by the Thing that now slouched toward the Minion. He wanted to slink away unnoticed but his body refused to move, paralyzed by the very horror his mind wanted to escape.

As fate would have it, at that moment his sight cleared. He took one look at the scene before him, a scene that would be forever burned into his mind.

There is a saying: "Never seek the attention of the immortal." Until now, he hadn't understood what that meant.

The trees around the clearing died, shriveled, fell. The ground under his feet shivered and a million tiny fissures shattered its surface. The very air itself thinned until he could hardly breathe. It was as if all creation drew back in horror, reluctant to even remain in the presence of the unclean

Being that came to grasp Azrael in its talons. The silence that hung around the scenario was more terrible than the loudest explosion, more soul-tearing than the harshest shriek of agony. The very fabric of his reality darkened until nothing remained but a single spear point of fear aimed directly at his mind, and miraculously his paralysis broke.

He fled into the safety of the forest, holding on to his sanity by the tiniest of threads.

* * *

Meeker was still shaking, eyes tightly closed. She jumped at a touch on her shoulder.

"Easy," Mason said, his speech slightly slurred from the swollen jaw and bleeding lips.

She glanced around hurriedly. From where they were, she could see most of the clearing. Besides the smoldering van and the still-burning limo, they were alone. It occurred to her she still clutched Jaelon's limp hand.

"Jaelon?" she said, peering into the woman's face.

Mason checked the Knight's neck for a pulse.

"She's alive," he told her, "but we need to get her to a hospital."

"How? The van's gone. She can't walk."

He started to answer but stopped at the sound of an approaching flyer. The smoke must have alerted the local authorities. They crouched under cover of the trees as the flyer circled the clearing then settled nearby. The doors of the flyer opened.

She almost cried out in relief when Populus and Martin spilled out of the machine.

12

After exchanging glad words with Martin, they flew for several hours, avoiding their pursuers handily using the modified comm unit. Meeker sat sadly most of the way. Using that remarkable healing ability they had evidenced before, Populus and Jaelon worked on the party's injuries.

When they were certain it was safe, they set down in a forested area in the plains of Missouri. As they set up camp, Martin filled them in on his escape.

"Then we commandeered the nearest flyer and Populus hacked the onboard computer in record time," he finished. "He got us clear before anyone knew what was really going on."

Mason shook his head, smiling. "Incredible."

"You don't know half of it," Martin went on. "On the way, we heard over the net that Nicholson had been shot dead in that little settlement about five miles from the cabin."

"It must have happened several hours before," Populus put in. "The local authorities are always late to arrive at anything that might be worse than a bar fight. I imagine they are afraid to get involved themselves."

"Did they say who killed him?"

"Party or parties unknown," Martin responded with a wry grin. "Evidently there were no witnesses."

"Poor Andrew," Meeker said softly.

The others refrained from comment. No one wanted to question her gentle spirit.

"Well," Martin said, "Azrael is gone. Nicholson is dead. News from Europe is looking good, with the Imperials giving ground and making concessions. Maybe we can take a few days off."

"I am afraid we must move on," Jaelon said, indicating herself and Populus. "Our task here is done, but we still have some work ahead in Europe." She looked at Mason. "It has been an honor."

Mason inclined his head. "For me as well."

"Have you given any thought to my question?" she asked.

Meeker and Martin looked from her to him, puzzled.

"I'm still working on it," he said.

"I see." The Knight fingered the pendant and looked at

the ground. "I understand."

He felt he should say something, but no words came.

"I hope you find your answer some day," she said.

There was a short, uncomfortable pause, then Populus clapped his hands together.

"Well, then, we must prepare for our journey," he said brightly.

"Where will you go from here?" Meeker asked. "Will we see you again?"

"I cannot answer either question just yet, my dear. The less you know, the better. However, I do hope our paths cross again soon."

"Aren't you going with us in the flyer?" Martin objected. "We can't just leave you here in the woods."

Populus laughed. "Mr. Martin, you need not concern yourself for us. We will manage."

"At least take some things from the flyer for your trip."

The Greek grinned and waved him ahead. "If you insist. After you."

They moved off toward the machine. Meeker walked to Jaelon and hugged her. A few hours of the same healing they had used to care for Nicholson's wounds brought Jaelon back to nearly full health. Mason had forgotten how self-sufficient the Knights were.

"Be safe," Meeker told her.

"I will do my best," was the reply. "And as for you, you have more courage and spirit than you realize. Listen to your heart. It will guide you truly always."

Meeker nodded and gave her a weak smile. "I will do my best."

Mason wandered off, leaving the women to talk. He found the shade of a nearby tree and dug out a long-overdue Montecristo, clamped it between his teeth. He took his time lighting the smoke, savoring the quiet of the moment after the frantic action of the last days. These few seconds of peace had become very precious to him, more so now than ever before.

There were still a few things to do. Populus would work with Meeker and Martin, preparing the follow-up attack. Eliminating Andlat Enterprises' presence in the network had stalled the Imperial advance, but it could recover quickly if the resources which built that network to begin with were still available. The last vestiges of Andlat Enterprises' computer programming capability had to be knocked out. When the Greek was satisfied, he too would be headed overseas.

Meeker's duty then would be to head to the New York megaplex and its ancient financial headquarters still referred to as "Wall Street," to preempt any defensive measures taken by The Enemy there.

What Martin would do, he could not say. The man was not the same person. Unsurprising, but still disconcerting. He'd known Martin for over a century. The Austrian was a kind of little brother to him. He felt both relief and sadness that he might never see the man again. It was an inevitable part of who and what they were.

Mason himself would shortly go to DC for some very bloody business indeed. For a moment, he was transported to a day in 1944, when he had been a bombardier over Germany. Once more, he was looking into the bomb sight at the munitions plant, the growl of the bomber loud in his ears. The sound of the bay doors whining open, the feel of the trigger in his fist. He squeezed, and the teardrop shapes fell away by the dozens.

They had not waited until the factory was closed and emptied of workers. Each munitions worker killed stalled the rebuild of the enemy's plant just that much more. In those days, there was no such thing as a "non-combatant." The enemy was the enemy, no matter who they were, military or civilian.

Then came French Indochina and the rise of Asian communism. Where the Western Marxists had failed, the Eastern succeeded. They convinced the world, through the new media of television and radio, that the people of a nation were separate from their government and their military was the bully arm of corruption. Mason ground his teeth at that, not for the first time. The Enemy had worked for decades to cut the connection between the governed and the governing. Only that way could they generate true despair and unchecked suffering. And their method was so successful it eventually found its way around the world; Africa, Australia, Europe, and finally the Americas. By 2020, the world had turned its back on anything other than what could be seen, tasted, smelled, heard, or felt. The ideas which had previously inspired men to divine heights of creativity were driven into the worlds of fantasy, no longer a part of "real life." For the members of the Army, who held fast to their knowledge of the Truth behind the principles of the Conflict, the lack of belief common to the general public was just another obstacle to overcome.

When a people are stripped of their belief in something greater than themselves, they lose the ability to resist those who promise them fulfillment of the vacuum left behind.

Mason, a soldier and strategist, understood this concept of conquering the mind first to make the conquest of the body easier. It continued to amaze him how The Enemy had accomplished it on such a scale, even if it had taken centuries to do.

Blood was still spilled in the Conflict. It was unavoidable and necessary because The Enemy refused to retreat before it came to bloodshed. Diplomacy might be entertained by The Enemy, but usually only as a delaying tactic to give themselves time to build strength enough to attack. The Army knew this, and accepted it because every moment free of active Conflict was used to advance the cause of peace. This balance had endured since the beginning, a cycle of life and death on a global scale that neither side knew how to break.

Mason contemplated the ash on the end of his cigar. Again he was struck by the comparison. This was what was left behind in the end, after all. Ashes. The ashes of civilizations, of cultures, of lives.

No more. It was time to bring this to an end. Whether it was just his part of it or the Conflict entire, it was time to bring this to an end. He could no longer simply be part of an ongoing struggle. He wanted to be part of the Solution.

He stood up and flicked the cigar away.

It was time to talk to Jaelon about that decision.

EPILOGUE

John Tripp sat rocking on the front porch of his farm house, listening to the frogs and crickets greet the coming night. The year's harvest was almost ready. The cloudless sky was just beginning to sparkle with the first stars. It was his favorite time, when the quiet of the evening slipped over the day's activities done. Somewhere a cow lowed a song at its calf. He sighed and closed his eyes, reveling in the caress of a cool breeze wafting from the trees that separated the house from the fields he'd tended these last fifteen years.

The aroma of cooking tickled his nose. He smiled as he thought of her, the woman who now shared the remaining days of his life. She never asked him about his past and he respected hers. They always looked forward, never back, except when entertaining her grandchildren. It was good to have the laughter of little ones echoing in the house. It was a hint of that sight he still cherished.

The memory of the Seraph was pure joy now. Gone was the terror and pain. Only the comfort remained. He scratched the stubble of his graying beard. Soon, now. Very soon he would see it again, this time in its full glory, without the restriction of mortal eyes.

The sound of footsteps on the porch stair brought him awake. He must have dozed, not to hear the man approach. The face was familiar but the aura of power and certainty was new to him. He smiled as he took the hand extended to him.

"It's good to see you again, my old friend," he said. "I suppose I should call you Knight Vernus now."

ABOUT THE AUTHOR

Born in San Antonio, Texas, David spent the majority of his formative years in Jacksonville, Florida. At the age of 16, his family moved to the Panama Canal Zone where David finished school and entered employment with the Department of Defense as a Powerhouse Electrician.

Hiring into the FAA, he returned with his wife and two daughters to the States and settled briefly in Gulfport, MS. A few years later, he moved to Memphis, TN, as an Air Traffic Controller for the Memphis ARTCC. There he remained until his retirement.

David's writing has appeared in numerous anthologies, magazines, webzines, and writer's sites. His work continues to appear on a regular basis through multiple publishing houses.

Transcend reality with Seventh Star Press!

On the following pages we would like to introduce you to some of our titles featuring Sword and Sorcery, Post-Apocalyptic Fantasy, Epic Fantasy, YA Fantasy, and more!

To get more information on Seventh Star Press and our titles, please visit:

www.seventhstarpress.com

or connect with us at:
www.twitter.com/7thstarpress
www.facebook.com/seventhstarpress

 SEVENTH STAR PRESS

Dystoptian Anthology Perfect Flaw
Now Available!

Softcover ISBN: 978-1-937929-11-4

eBook ISBN: 978-1-937929-13-8

Readers everywhere are invited to experience adventures of a dystopian nature in the anthology Perfect Flaw, from editor Robin Blankenship! Featuring seventeen speculative fiction tales, spanning many genres, Perfect Flaw explores the subject of societies gone wrong. From "utopian" societies masking an underlying controlled state, to stories of people fighting back against repression, in hopes of a better world, the flaws that create a dystopian atmosphere are brought to light. Thought-provoking and entertaining, Perfect Flaw will be a welcome addition to any reader's collection of dystopian literature.

Make sure you own the first two volumes of the
The Angelkiller Triad!.

H. David Blalock

The Angelkiller Triad
Featuring cover art and interior illustrations by
the award-winning Matthew Perry

Softcover ISBN:

9781937929732

eBook ISBN:

9781937929749

Softcover ISBN:

9780983740230

eBook ISBN:

9780983740285

A paranormal thrill ride from Eric Garrison! Four 'Til Late is Book One of the Road Ghosts Trilogy!

Softcover: 978-1-937929-22-0

eBook: 978-1-937929-23-7

In Four 'Til Late, amateur ghost hunter Brett and his friends Gonzo, Jimbo, and Liz are on a road trip with dangerous detours, dreadful dreams and dire warnings. But that won't keep them from reaching their goal: New Orleans. Along the way they discover that some spirits leave you with more than a hangover and regrets. Can they get there in one piece, or will they be stopped and rest in peace? The bags are packed, the engine's running. Turn up the radio and get moving because the road ghosts are waiting, and it's Four 'Til Late.

Virtual Blue from R.J. Sullivan!

Softcover ISBN: 978-1-937929-32-9

eBook ISBN: 978-1-937929-33-6

Did you ever wish you could escape to a virtual world? What if you could...but then couldn't get out? Two years after her deadly clash with a vengeful ghost, Fiona "Blue" Shaefer still can't shake off the trauma of that night. Moving to New York with her father didn't help. Neither did absorbing herself in her college classes. Not even her poetry provided the solace it once did. She convinces herself that ending her relationship with Eugene "Chip" Farren, her long-distance boyfriend and final tie to the horrors of that night, might bring the closure she needs. Blue travels to Bloomington to break the news to Chip in person, but her timing couldn't be any worse. The Sisters of Baalina, vengeful cultists who practice a new form of "techno-magic," have targeted Chip's multi-player videogame as the perfect environment to cast a dangerous spell to free a demoness from the very pits of hell. In the process, their plan may trap Blue in a prison of the mind with no locks, no bars, and no escape.

Hellscapes, Volume 1
Venture through the infernal, where
angels fear to tread!

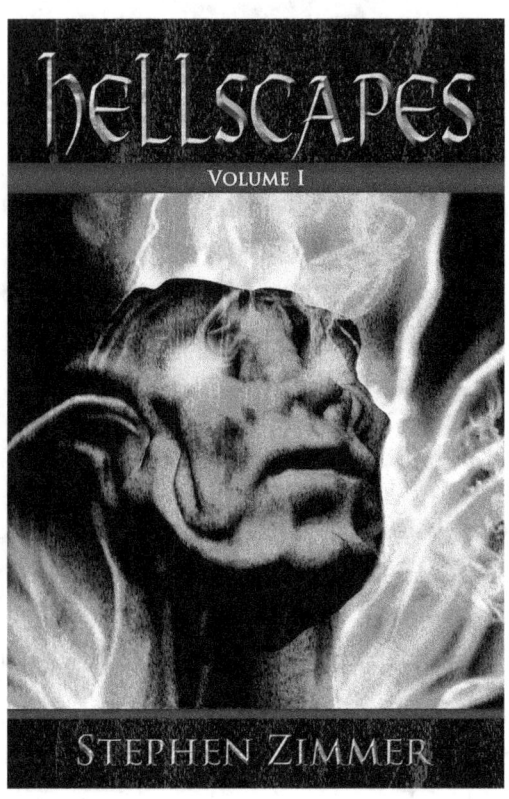

From Stephen Zimmer, a new
horror series set in realms where the
inhabitants experience the ultimate
nightmare!

softcover ISBN: 978-1-937929-36-7
eBook ISBN: 978-1-937929-37-4

Now Available from Seventh Star Press,
the horror stylings of

Michael West!

Trade Paperback ISBN: 9780983740209
eBook ISBN: 9780983740216

Trade Paperback ISBN: 9781937929718
eBook ISBN: 9781937929725

Trade Paperback ISBN: 9781937929954
eBook ISBN:9781937929831

Trade Paperback ISBN: 978-1-937929-18-3
eBook ISBN: 978-1-937929-19-0

Urban Fantasy from John F. Allen!

Meet Ivory Blaque!

Softcover: 978-1-937929-16-9

eBook: 978-1-937929-17-6

In The God Killers, the first book of The God Killers Legacy, former professional art thief Ivory Blaque is hired to procure a pair of antique pistols and gets much more than she bargained for when several attempts are made on her life.

Her client turns out to be a shadowy government agent who reveals that she is descended from a race of immortals, and that the pistols are linked to her unique heritage and the special psychic gifts she possesses. He uses the memory of her father to guilt her into working for him.

Ivory eventually gives in to his request, and in return, he presents her with her father's journal, which was written in an unbreakable code. Bishop believes that she is the only one capable of breaking the code and unlocking the plans of the vampire hierarchy. But when the city's top vampire is a sexy incubus with an attraction for her and she's assigned a hot new lycan enforcer to protect her, she finds herself caught between two sets of rock hard abs.

To regain her autonomy, clear her name, unlock the secrets of her past, and protect the lives of those closest to her, Ivory must play along with the forces trying to manipulate her. Ivory's life is rapidly spiraling out of control and headed for an explosive conclusion which she just might not survive.

Now available from Seventh Star Press! The Rising Dawn Saga, a series that explores the dystopian and the apocalyptic from author

Stephen Zimmer

Book One: The Exodus Gate
Softcover ISBN: 9780615267470
eBook ISBN: 9780982565674

Book Two: The Storm Guardians
Softcover ISBN: 9780982565636
eBook ISBN: 9780982565681

Book Three: The Seventh Throne
Softcover ISBN: 9780983740247
eBook ISBN: 9780983740223